Egg SS
Eggers, Paul.
How the water feels :
  stories $ 19.95
1st ed.

How
the
Water
Feels

ALSO BY PAUL EGGERS

Saviors

Stories by Paul Eggers

How
the
Water
Feels

SOUTHERN METHODIST
UNIVERSITY PRESS
Dallas

This collection of stories is a work of fiction. Names, characters, places, and incidents are either the product of the author's imagination or are used fictitiously.

Requests for permission to reproduce material
from this work should be sent to:
    Rights and Permissions
    Southern Methodist University Press
    PO Box 750415
    Dallas, Texas 75275-0415

Jacket photograph by Phong L. Tran, with special thanks to Anh Thong Le
Jacket design: Tom Dawson and Teresa W. Wingfield
Text design: Teresa W. Wingfield

LIBRARY OF CONGRESS CATALOGING-IN-PUBLICATION DATA
Eggers, Paul.
    How the water feels : stories / by Paul Eggers. — 1st ed.
        p.   cm.
    Contents: How the water feels — Substitutes — Anything you want, please —
Proof — Leo, chained — The big gift — The year five — A private space.
    ISBN 0-87074-473-9 (alk. paper)
        1. Northwest, Pacific — Social life and customs — Fiction.
2. Malaysia — Social life and customs — Fiction.   3. Refugee camps —
Fiction.   4. Refugees — Fiction.   I. Title.

Printed in the United States of America on acid-free paper

10   9   8   7   6   5   4   3   2   1

For Ellen

Acknowledgments

Early versions of these stories originally appeared in the following periodicals:"How the Water Feels" in *Granta*; "Substitutes" in *Prairie Schooner*; "Anything You Want, Please" in *Northwest Review*; "Proof" in *The Quarterly*; "Leo, Chained" in *The William and Mary Review*; "The Big Gift" in *Meridian*; and "The Year Five" in *Quarterly West*.

Contents

How
the
Water
Feels

Mr. Luc, originally of Saigon, conducted his campwide rat pogrom so thoroughly the kids were reduced to throwing rocks at each other. Some boys got beaned, and Mr. Luc, the most responsible Viet I knew in the Bidong Island refugee camp, blamed himself and went around shelter to shelter, apologizing to all their parents, more than twenty families. This was Mr. Luc's way. Before getting on a boat out of Vietnam, he had been a colonel with the South Vietnamese army. Even now, stateless and dependent, another Viet biding his time in Malaysian territory, he wore a dashing yellow scarf imprinted with the name of his old regiment.

I was the UN education adviser, the camp's English teacher. Mr. Luc was my refugee assistant. I had picked him myself, struck by his earnestness, and would give him occasional gifts, whatever I could scrounge. Mr. Luc and I were two of a kind. I understood his need to be forgiven—he had let the camp down, he said—and I even understood the state of mind that made him, after a day of brush-offs from the boys' parents, walk into the island's Zone C school the next morning and root around the UN educational-supplies closet and, without asking permission, drag a filthy visual aid, a mannequin, down to the beach to wash clean. What I could not do that morning was clear his supply-closet foray with the camp's Malaysian security fucks. Mr. Luc had acted on his own. If only I had known he was going to take the mannequin, I could have stopped refugee-camp logic from taking over.

I felt so guilty I went to Mr. Luc that night to apologize. He told me the mannequin had been dirty. Rats had gnawed through its feet, and my predecessor, Barbara somebody, had smeared THIS IS AN ARM, LESSON 21 on one shoulder in Magic Marker. It had needed cleansing, he said—"Unclean, yeah? Mr. Joe, I can say *unclean?*" This was how we spoke: a kind of code, intimate as lovers. In the classroom, he tried hard to make me look good. He was aware of the roles we had been assigned. His was to appease, to act as factotum to the powerful forces that determined his fate. So he asked me language questions, softballs a child could hit: me, the adviser, the American, the giant.

It was November 1980, and the beast was about to rise from the ocean. What was my guilt compared to that? The Malaysians were threatening to close the Bidong Island camp before the end of the year. They said the boat people weren't their responsibility alone. They said somebody, somewhere, better open their doors—or else. Since October, a battalion of Malaysian Rangers had been bivouacked on the mainland, an hour away. If they came, they would come hard and fast, with weapons. The boat people, all thirty thousand of them, would be towed back out in their leaky wrecks into the roaring water and cut adrift. Helicopters would come for us UN workers, and we would soar over the tiny island, strapped in tight, too ashamed to speak.

And still, Mr. Luc let me sit on his cardboard and scrape the mud from my sandals and correct his English. I loved him so much for it I couldn't look him in the face.

He told me what had happened. The head fuck, Captain Rahim, had thought the mannequin was a real person at first. Specifically, me. There were about eighty fucks in camp, a hodgepodge of local militia and police, and Rahim was the nastiest: a rat-faced village boy who thought all the Viets were communist agents. That morning, he had been patrolling the Zone C beach when he saw Mr. Luc kneeling in the water, caressing what appeared to be a naked white man. Rahim didn't know squat about what we kept in the supply closet. After he rescued the mannequin, a bunch of Viets laughed at him. Rahim made a run at them, but they just disappeared and hooted from behind trees. And then he walked back and rough-talked Mr. Luc. Rahim can't have known for sure the mannequin was a supply item—the thing could have just washed up on the beach—but he was so mad it didn't make any difference. It was white-bastard colored, so it must belong to Mr. Luc's white-bastard adviser.

That afternoon, Rahim fidgeted outside the wire fence of the UN compound for a while, then opened the gate and confronted me. "No *sir*," I said in my best military-sarcastic voice. "Don't know anything. I just teach English." I was only half-lying: I hadn't seen Mr. Luc all day. I was sick, shiny with fever sweat, and had been sleeping in my bungalow. Still, I had a clear picture of the item: the stovepipe plastic legs, the phony mustache and nose, the spooky, blank eyes. I had never touched the thing. It gave me the creeps. How, I wondered, would one teach with it?

Rahim just stood there, screwing up his little rat face, and I folded my arms. I figured if the head fuck cared so much, I had an obligation to mess with him. The Malaysians owned the soil, but the UN paid the bills. I was jacked. I could feel my hair stand on end. I was staring Rahim down, watching his nasty little face getting rattier and rattier, while behind him a crowd of Viets was gathering by the fence. Any time we stirred in the compound, they leaned against the wire and stared, as though they were watching a play. I saw them whispering to each other. I imagined them applauding my stand: *That Mr. Joe, he's some guy.*

"Mannequin?" I said, loudly. "What mannequin? I don't know about any mannequin."

"How you cannot know who this is?" he said. He was holding one of its plastic fingers and waved it at me.

Who this is. I smelled victory.

"You mean, 'Whose this is' or 'To whom this belongs,'" I said. I towered over him. I could see the curry stains on his little bus-driver hat.

His face quivered a second, and I sensed him withdraw. Somewhere under that hat, a decision was being made. He turned and waved for his Viet assistant, who suddenly appeared from behind the crowd, opened the gate and entered forbidden ground, dragging the rest of the mannequin behind him.

Rahim trotted back and huddled with the man. Viets were now two deep outside the wire. The assistant looked worried. But Rahim said, "Okay, okay," and clapped him hard on the back. They set to work. They yanked off the head. They popped off the legs—Rahim holding the torso, his assistant tugging—and they bent back the hands. The crowd was laughing and pointing. Rahim couldn't get one of the arms off, so he had his assistant wiggle it back and forth until it stuck straight up.

When they were done, they left the parts in the sand. They stood there a moment, hands on their hips, as though they were viewing something monstrous. I could see the hollow cavity where the head had been.

The way the Viets parted for Rahim at the gate and all the way down the beach into Zone C, you could tell he was still pissed. A few hours later, Rahim accused Mr. Luc of trying to steal the mannequin. Around dinner, just as the sky was exploding with color, the fucks rousted Mr. Luc from his lean-to and shaved his head and whacked him around with a rattan.

Roland was the only one who accused me but, coming from him, it meant something. I admired him. He was a fat tub, a Canadian, but he kept a cool head. He was a straight arrow. On the bungalow porch, he sidled up and said, "You're not simply you here, Joe. You're a *symbol*. You got to show some sense."

I didn't argue.

"You piss off Rahim," he said, "and the fucks get on the short-wave to the mainland. The Rangers are licking their chops. They're just looking for a reason to come."

"Tell me something I don't know," I said.

"Okay, hero. Maybe we ought to have Rahim give *you* a haircut and massage."

"Hey, look," I said.

"This isn't your first screw-up."

We were both quiet for a while, and he started scratching his arm, waiting for me to speak. I wouldn't. Then he gave me an example—a hypothetical, he said, though he was looking straight at me. He said it was like this, it was like if someone, you know, let's say *you*, gave a shot of Johnnie Walker to a Viet; it wasn't just that person breaking a fuck rule, it was Uncle Sam and Aunt Geneva and Queen Victoria, the money and the arrogance of the white-bastard world. The Malaysians, he said, didn't like that.

He said it as though he was teaching me a big lesson.

"Hey," I said. "You got something to say to me, say it. I make mistakes, all right? I've been sick."

"That's no excuse," he said. "What you feel doesn't matter."

"I've been sick. I'm not making excuses. I'm just saying I'm flesh and blood. Now give it a rest."

He wouldn't. "You got to play the game right," he said.

I looked out at the ocean. "You see that?" I said, pointing. "Way over there?"

He shaded his eyes and looked. Then he started shaking his head. "I'm here to tell you, man, the Viets don't want *you*." He pointed at me. "Think about it. They want what you *represent*. Somebody important sent you, didn't they? That's what they want."

"I do my job. I'm not dead weight."

"The Viets don't love you, white boy," he said. He shook his head. "You're nothing. *Nada*, yes? Zero. But what you mean to the Viets is, 'Hey, someone real out there gives a shit.'"

"I do my job," I said.

"Someone real," he said. "Uncle Sam. God. Some cousin in California. Not you. Someone who can get them out of here. So start teaching English."

I walked away.

He called after me. "The Rangers come," he said, "then what good are we? Huh?"

I had classes to teach, and on the way I stopped in to see Mr. Luc and give him some baby milk I had taken from the shipment at the depot. He was grateful. He gave me cardboard to sit on and put a pot of brown water on the fire pit to boil. We didn't say much. He had a welt on his back, so I gave him my tube of antiseptic cream. I had some blue paper left over from a lesson, so I gave that to him too, and a pen and a Malaysian coin and a stick of gum and a paper clip. I emptied my pockets for him. I would have given him a thousand bucks if I'd had it, and a plane ticket straight to L.A. I would have shielded him with my body and taken him to the dock and hitched a ride on the supply boat all the way to the mainland. I would have jawed with the fucks and waved my passport around and screamed in their faces with a bullhorn. I would have put Mr. Luc on a bus to Kuala Lumpur and wiped his ass and cut up his meat and carried him onto the plane and flown him myself all the way across the Pacific.

Mr. Luc and I drank weak tea out of severed 7-Up cans. When you rolled up the flour-sack wall of his lean-to, all you saw was ocean. When the Rangers came, they would first appear out there, in bristling water, in a bee-swarm of engines. The whole island would stand there and stare, whispering that the beast had come. For a week now, kids had been lining the outcrop, watching the ocean, pointing. They held tightly wound palm fronds to blow like trumpets.

No one knew if the Rangers would actually come. We listened to our guts. We let the rumors hang in the air. We'd sit on someone's bunk and drink Johnnie Walker. We'd get sloppy drunk. A Viet would always be rattling something off through the camp speakers, so we'd start to talk real loud, nonstop.

This much was true: Ranger fucks had been speedboating out once a week, just walking around, scoping things. I made sure I got noticed. I wore my powder-blue T-shirt. When the Rangers saw me, my sandy hair and sunburned neck, they saw white-bastard UNHCR. They'd nod and grin like village boys, and they'd push through the Viets to shake my hand and show off their Form 5 English. And when they touched me, when their eyes roamed over my white skin, when they smelled my diet of meat, what was shining in their eyes was Neil Armstrong on the moon, and John Wayne, and redheads without bras, and so much money you could take an airplane ride once a week. I *was* the white-bastard world. No me, no symbol. I had power. I made the Rangers think twice. I'd say, "It's under control here, yeah? It is *under control*," and they'd smile like schoolgirls. "No problem," they'd say, and I'd grab the nearest Viet and put my arms around him. *Bye-bye*, we'd say, *bye-bye, bye-bye*.

Roland was just the radiologist in the camp hospital, but since the doctors were always shorthanded, he was allowed to join in the glory work and came to lunch with blood on his shirt. He loved to talk about how many cc's of this or that he was shooting into people's veins. Every surface in his room was covered with folders of X rays and mysterious, smelly specimens in capped plastic cups.

But now I realized: he thought if you didn't have blood on your shirt, you weren't really there.

I said, "That's some superior stink coming from you."

"Burn victim," he said. He was carrying a box of tubes and shook them at me like noodles. "Some kid fell down a well, only it was dry and they were using it as a fire pit. The smell gets on you."

"*Superior* stink."

"Mr. Joe," he said. "Can you spell 'superior'?"

"You want some?" I said. "Let's get it on. Right now."

But he wasn't listening. A cherry was coming in on the morning supply-boat run, and he had heard it was a nurse's aide from New Zealand. He wanted the office to look sharp.

Cherries: we talked as though we were out on jungle patrol. Some nights I fantasized about walking single-file in a combat squad, sneaking past the tarp-and-sapling shanties where the Viets slept in hammocks or on cardboard. How much would a rucksack weigh me down? How would a flak jacket feel against my stomach? I secured the perimeter, I patrolled the ville. The air smelled like mud, even when the stars were out and a nice breeze was coming in, and then I'd look out across the Zone C footpath and see Viets in running shorts hustle someone off, and I knew they were going to cut him for something he had done on the boat trip over.

You couldn't blame the refugees. In the South China Sea, they could float for months. Sometimes, when the Thais pulled alongside, the women jumped in the water to drown. The sun and ocean bleached the refugees like rags. They fought over water jugs. When the boats came in, you could smell what had happened.

The stories I heard about some of those boat journeys made me so angry I never stopped a cut-party. If I'd wanted to, I could have plowed through the Viets and pulled the victim to safety. Malay and white, we could do that. I could have put my arm around the man's waist, and he would have been safe as the Pope buckled up in his Popemobile. But I wouldn't. I was so angry just thinking about what he must have done, I'd say, "You hustle his ass. You take him out and you make him *pay*."

After lunch, a few of us waited on the dock for the cherry and said funny things to the Viet kids playing on the engine blocks sticking out of the shallow water. The monsoons had started early. Some nights the rain was so heavy it sounded like rocks falling from the sky, and later we would hear the Viets in their lean-tos swearing and scooping out the mud in plastic buckets and throwing it onto the footpaths. When it wasn't raining, the sun came out and just stayed there, right in your face, and after a while the Viet kids looked like they had cracks all over their bodies from where the mud had dried, so they waded out among the debris and blue-gills to wet themselves up.

The cherry was Sally Hindermann. The first thing she did was point at the muddy beach and say, "Jesus, it looks like Play-Doh." I ignored her comment. She was tired, and by the look on her face a little scared. She had gotten seasick on the way over, she said, but had thought to bring plastic baggies and just zipped the mess up and threw it overboard.

"Good thinking," said Roland.

I was searching for a kind response, some lie, an act of gracious-ness. "Hey," I said. "Okay. How about that."

It turned out Roland had got it wrong: Sally was an English teacher, not a nurse's aide. She had a masters in teaching English as a second language from some college in Vermont, and from the moment the pillhouse fuck at the end of the dock waved us through and down the steps onto the beach, I could feel her watching my every move. That afternoon I took her for an English-teaching tour in my Zone F intermediate class. I carried around an oversized lesson planner and attendance book and stood ramrod straight on the podium the Viets had built for me. I did what I knew. I had a sponge for an eraser, and I shouted over the loudspeaker racket. I took off my watch and one of my shoes and said, "What's this?" and the Viets shouted their answers back at me. I pointed: shirt, ground, girl, boy, podium. "What's this?" I said. "What's this?" The class shouted back. The whole hour, Sally scraped mud off her ankles with a notepad and played with her hair.

"What's your background?" she said during break.

"Peace Corps," I said. "Some outside teaching here and there. Hey, you're the expert. No contest."

I thought I sounded pretty magnanimous: the *real* expert, the guy who knew the ropes, making the newcomer feel at ease. But

9

from the way she was looking at me, I could tell the computer in her head was going full tilt.

She had a little smile that kept quivering at the ends. I knew she had another face she wasn't sure she could show yet. That other face would accuse me soon. It would ferret out facts.

The facts: summers fishing in Alaska; two years of community college in Wassau; my friend Bud, in Records and Admission, he of the electric eraser and drugged-out, anything-for-you access to files. I had been in Peace Corps Malaysia all right, but I had quit during training and gone north, doping around Bangkok for a couple of years, teaching coconut-head English to tour guides. I figured if I could speak it, I could teach it. I was drunk with the ease of it. The tour guides couldn't read white people. I'd laugh at nothing— T-shirts, dogs, restaurant names—and tell them it was American humor. They told me I looked like Vic Morrow on *Combat!*, and I told them I knew him. I had them read the *Bangkok Post* to me, and I jumped all over their pronunciation. Sometimes, if they were doing too well, I'd make it up. "*Goov*-ernment," I'd say. "Try it again. 'The American *goo*vernment.'" I printed up certificates. A guy in Changmai had official seals. I made money; I drank iced coffee in restaurants all day and hung around the basement bar at the Opera Hotel at night.

I hung around, and the boat people came swarming into the ocean, drowning by the thousands. "They are *drooning*," I told my tour guides. "Say it again. Drooning." They scowled at the word in the *Bangkok Post* and repeated after me, chanting, and one of them, a joker, went *glub-glub* and shook his arms in the air, and then something came over me, some jolt, some black shame, and I smacked my hand on the table and said we were through, and everyone filed out because they could see I was shaking. Later, I lied my way onto the island, through a Pakistani with the UN, a bar crawler. "You," he said, sweating with beer. "You are teaching English, isn't it? Expert, yes?" The Opera Hotel bar had mirrors on the walls, and the black gauze netting on the ceiling was heavy with twinkling bulbs; the bar girls clicked their plastic number-tags, and in the fluorescent light my face was green. I nodded to the Paki. I knew where the conversation was going and I lied to him.

I lied because I was ashamed, but more than that: I lied because I saw what I was becoming. I was aimless, slick in a petty way, my spirit seeping out of me in small gasps. At the Opera Hotel, I got in altercations, little come-ons, mostly with Germans in cowboy hats, roustabouts from the oil-drilling platforms. They were sloppy and fat and unshaven. They ate chicken wrapped in tinfoil and made the bar girls suck the bones. I'd say, "Zo, vere ist der Führer? Ist *you* der Führer? Ist you?" Usually they just looked away. But when they were in the mood, they'd say something real insulting in German, and I'd leap up and be ready. I'd hear myself breathe like a horse and I'd have my hand tight around a bottle. "Vere ist der Führer? Vere? Who ist he? Ist he you? You?" I'd shake and pound the counter and try to move my legs, only all I could do was sway. "Vere ist he?" I'd say, pushing, straining, my ears popping, ready to explode, only I couldn't do anything and I just had to stand there with sweat pouring down my face until the bar girls came over and cooed they loved me until I sat back down.

Bidong was a thousand redemptions, every moment an ecstasy: a girl rubbing her gums, a man coughing into a bucket, a chainsaw whirring through plywood. In dreams I heard Viet-talk, little musical scales, only what they were saying was *Mr. Joe, Mr. Joe.*

But Sally didn't know that. All she saw was me pointing and shouting "What's this?" Later that day, she did a lesson with my intermediate students. They sat on coconut-tree planks lashed together with pink raffia string; the sugar-bag walls billowed in the breeze. Sally had them laughing inside five minutes. She put them into groups, had them holding conversations. She did incredible things with her fingers, popping them up and down to represent words in sentences; she didn't yell in their ears. I couldn't believe how professional she was, how good.

"Mr. Joe," my students said. "She is *very* good."

"Very good, Mr. Joe."

"I am speaking English, Mr. Joe."

"You are very wonderful, Miss Sally," said my best student. The man smiled so big he didn't look like the same person I saw every day. In a few weeks, they would all be looking at me with faces I didn't know.

So when we had to interview a new batch of arrivals for placements, I told Sally to ask, "How many children do you have?" I told her the Viets love to talk about their kids, that it was the best question, that you could get a real good gauge of their English level from asking it. I told her it was the test I always used.

The first woman had iron-gray hair in a bun.

"How many children do you have?" said Sally. The woman looked at Sally a moment, then at the floor.

I leaned over. "This batch here just got in," I said. My voice was raspy and quavering. "Their boat was out there a couple weeks."

Sally nodded.

"So she's tired," I said, real nice. "Try again."

"I *know*," Sally said. She smiled at the woman and locked on to her with her eyes.

"How many children do you have?" she said.

Nobody in the line moved; you could see them craning their necks forward to see what was taking so long. "I have four," the woman said, but then her shoulders were shaking. "Thai pirate kill one." Her voice started cracking. "Three daughter, one son." Then the Viets in line started whispering. They got this hard look on their faces, and one of them said, "No," real nasty, in Sally's direction.

Sally looked at me with fury. She didn't say a word, but she didn't have to. One of the Viets started yelling in Viet-talk. He got out of line and walked down the hill; others followed.

Later, I walked with Sally down to the Zone C beach, where the garbage was piled to your waist. At night you could shine your flashlight and see the beach shimmer with so many rats you thought you were looking at the ocean. The *whole beach*, I said. That many rats. I said it gruffly, with authority, as if to say: This is how it is, this is what's real, get used to it. I talked like I was showing her the ropes, preparing her for life on Bidong.

Ralph the Scottish engineer came up to us, and I turned to him, grateful for the company. Ralph was responsible for sanitation, but all he had were grannies carrying wicker baskets and farmers who didn't mind moving sewage along with hookpoles. I could hear the plastic and cans rustling offshore; black clods drifted in the foam like seaweed. I started to tremble. I wanted to fall to my knees. I wanted to say, "I am the most savage fuck on this island."

But I didn't. There was a twitter, some little spark of hope that wouldn't let me say what I knew was true. Because if I said it, then what could we do? Any of us—Viet, white, and fuck.

Sally and Ralph were looking at me. "Your Garbageness," I said to Ralph, holding my nose. "This just stinks to high heaven."

Sally and I split up the schools: she had Zones A to D, I had E to G.

"Why don't I come by Zone F today?" she said. It was so hot we were itchy. I was in running shorts and my powder-blue T-shirt. Sally had on a brown sundress; her arms were full of books. "I've got some Longman Series books," she said. "We could do some team-teaching."

"Is that like tag-team wrestling?" I said. "Crossover toehold, then I come in and put on the Sleeper?"

"Oh Joe," she said.

"I mean these Viets, they're wiry all right, but I'm the crowd favorite."

"Oh Joe," she said. She held her books over her head like an umbrella and squinted. "How are you, really? And your Mr. Luc. Is he doing well?"

"I don't know about well, but he's doing Miss Thuy, I think."

It was a good answer, a sleepy little quip to end the conversation and get on with the day. She knew I wasn't going to talk to her about Mr. Luc; what she wanted was the satisfaction of having asked and of having played her role well. She ordered people around and wore lipstick and curled her hair—she pretended it was natural, but the Viet washerwomen showed me her curlers. I saw she was a liar. She was playing Hotlips to my Hawkeye. Her other face, the one that would accuse me some day, denounce me—I could keep that face from surfacing by being Hawkeye, throwing lame one-liners her way, keeping her little smile quivering at the ends. Hawkeye was simple. He said *yuck-yuck* so he wouldn't have to say *boo-hoo*, and he called his cowardice black humor. Sally ate it up. Every time she put her hands on her hips and said, "Now Joe, not everything's funny," and pouted around, I knew she would be in her bungalow that night, the BBC on her shortwave, writing airgrams about how wacky we got, how tragic our smiles, how hard-nosed our love, how good we were.

Up the hill in my Zone F school, I saw one of the little high-keeled clinker boats come around the westward side, putt-putting. We all ran out of class and looked; the loudspeakers started going crazy with Viet-talk, and you could hear people shouting. The planks of the boat were so worn they looked like straw. I could see arms waving. The Viets came straight from Vietnam in boats I wouldn't take around a lake. They would bring aboard cast-iron cooking pots and cases of Coca-Cola. Most didn't know how to swim; they listened for the tide tables on the Voice of America and took their chances.

I ran on down with everyone else, dignified as I could, but when I reached the dock I was sweaty and spattered with mud; the beach had hold of my ankles; I was as slow as a swimmer, one stroke at a time. The beach was already thick with Viets. They were still running in from the tree line behind our compound, and kids were standing on the engine blocks, cheering. All I could see was black hair and brown legs, a rippling brown, T-shirted sea, but I wanted to be there when the boat putt-putted to the dock, so I stuck out my white arms to let everyone see who was coming and cut through the crowd.

Mr. Luc was waving to me a stone's throw away. I pushed closer. "American, American," I said, and people turned sideways to let me through. I waved back to Mr. Luc, shouting greetings, but then we were stuck. The beach was so packed up front, there was no room to move. Up around the dock steps, I heard splashing. People were being pushed by the crowd into the water.

"Ever been in a riot?" said Roland. He rammed me from behind with his elbow, but it wasn't his fault; we were all holding onto the shoulders of the person in front, leaning forward with the crowd and drawing back, trying to keep our balance.

I couldn't see much. The fucks were out in force, but they were just going through the motions, banging truncheons on the pilings to let everyone know they were there. Two of them stood on the dock steps holding their M-16s. Some other fucks and Vietnamese security with special white bracelets milled around. A Viet was lashing the docking rope around a pillar. The boat was rocking, bumping against the dock, and the pilothouse window had been smashed. One of the fucks dragged a portable ladder and a blanket from the pillhouse and started helping people off, single file. They were dirty and scared. Captain Rahim, wearing his little bus-driver hat, chivvied them along. The last one off, a woman, was wearing a blanket. Her hair was wild; she was trembling so hard she stumbled a little on the last rung, and for a moment you could see she was naked underneath.

"Now we know," said Roland.

I didn't say anything. I was chewing the inside of my cheek.

"Thai pirates got her," he said.

"I *know*."

The way he said *got her* made me shout it.

One of the fucks ran up and lent her his arm, which seemed to me really decent, except that Roland pointed to him and shouted, "The fuck has a hard-on."

I looked, but couldn't see. "Where?"

"Right *there*," he said, pointing. "What do you mean 'where'? You think it's on his head?"

"You're full of it," I said. "He's helping her."

"You don't want to see, okay."

I stooped my shoulders and frowned, zeroing in on the fuck. He was snapping his fingers at one of the Viet security guys, who ran into the pillhouse and came out with another blanket.

"He doesn't have one," I said.

"Hey," he said, cupping his hand. "You want to defend him, go ahead."

"If it's not there, it's *not there*," I said. "And it's *not there*."

The naked woman collapsed, and a couple of the Viets in line started walking over to her, while the fucks clapped their hands as if commanding genies to disappear and chased them back.

Some Viet security ran into the pillhouse and came out with a stretcher.

Mr. Luc squeezed over and greeted me politely, but I could tell he was agitated. His voice was pinched, as if he was about to get the dry heaves.

"Mr. Joe," he said, touching my arm. "The woman is very afraid, yeah. You can do? Yeah."

You can do, as in, Why can't you get out there and summon white jinns and make this go away?

I held on tight to the shoulders of the man in front. "Mr. Luc. I'm sorry. I would if I could." I could hear my heart pounding; I was shouting over the crowd.

"The stretcher's there," I said. "They're lifting her now."

"You're not looking right," said Roland.

"He *doesn't have one*," I said.

"No?" said Roland. He paused a moment. "Okay. Okay. I was

wrong." He grabbed hold of my shoulders. "Who does? Maybe it's you, huh?"

"Shut up," I said, and I looked down. I looked down, just for a moment, not even moving my head. I looked down just to make sure.

Roland and Mr. Luc followed my eyes and then looked at me.

"My mistake," said Roland. "Sorry."

Mr. Luc's face clamped shut. His shoulders hunched.

The crowd was shouting out questions in Vietnamese: "What province are you from?" "How many days did you sail?" "Do you know my town?" Roland put his hand on my shoulder and talked into my ear. He said he didn't mean it. He said he was just upset. He was asking me to forgive him. Mr. Luc's elbow jabbed me hard in the ribs, but when I looked over he was drifting away, caught from behind in a current of people. He didn't look back. The current caught me, and I could hear people yelling, snapping at each other, and we all stumbled forward, closing in on the dock, where I could see the fucks raising their truncheons, warning people away from the steps. I would ride the current, feel the hands pushing from behind, and at the last second I would grab one of the fucks by the arm, I would shout in his face and start pulling at his shirt until he brought his truncheon down and made me bite my tongue and tumble into the water, splashing, blood speckling my shirt, and I would sink to my knees, yelling from my gut.

But that's not what happened. What happened was, the pushing stopped. Just like that. We all held on to each other's shoulders, breathing hard, waiting. The Viets started talking softly, whispering, calming each other down. You could hear the little clinker boat creaking in the water. Roland was breathing behind me, rubbing my shoulders. Captain Rahim had his bullhorn out and started yelling at the crowd and waving his bus-driver hat around. I smelled a whiff of mercurochrome; one of the Viet security men was dabbing a cotton ball on the naked woman's head. I heard seagulls, and in front of me, the tiny waves rolled onto the sand. I saw Mr.

Luc and sidled my way around until I was staring him hard in the face and told him I had something wrong inside. I pointed to my chest and screwed up my mouth. I roared at him.

Later, after the crowd had disappeared, Mr. Luc and I walked down the beach. He stopped to wash the dirt off his arms and looked at me with a question on his face, and I told him I would just have a bucket bath in the compound. I told him Miss Sally would be teaching the lessons tomorrow. I stood a few paces back, a decent distance, while he frothed the water. When he was finished, he was clean.

Substitutes

"My husband the refugee," Bridget said, and who could blame her? The way Owen was going on, you'd think Jesus Himself was playing chess up in Vancouver, not Bobby Fischer. "Robert James Fischer," Owen crowed. He looked at her sharply: "The grandmaster? The heir apparent?" "I *know*," she said, and spread out the road map onto the table. All you had to do was turn on the TV to know Bobby Fischer was in the Pacific Northwest. His quarterfinals match was taking place just across the Canadian border, in a hushed Vancouver auditorium. According to what she had overheard Owen say on the phone, the result of the match was a foregone conclusion. Bobby would win handily—his opponent, the Russian grandmaster and concert pianist Mark Taimanov, was possibly the weakest of the challengers—then advance into the semis and the finals, then battle the mighty Boris Spassky for the world chess crown.

"Bobby's going to kill him today," Owen said. Apparently he wasn't done upsetting her. The use of a stranger's first name, the brutal language: it was goading and even frightening.

"And now the ugliness truly starts," she said, smoothing the crinkled map with her hand. There. That shut him up. She heard him say then in a nicer voice he was just clowning. She looked up at him crossly, half expecting to see his jaw set in defiance, but saw he had indeed regained his equilibrium. Just like that. The symptoms of his chess fever (the term, his invention, struck her now as evasive) had vanished, and in place of his stony mouth and narrowed, gun-slit eyes was the face of the Owen she had seen at breakfast, or rather glimpsed in passing as she ate alone, a face serene and open as a parasol.

"And were you clowning about being in Bobby's presence too?" She put bunny ears around "Bobby's presence," an inflammatory gesture, she knew—he was sensitive to mocking—but she had a right to let him know how much he had alarmed her with his outburst.

"No, I'm completely nuts."

"Please don't do that."

"Well then, what do you think? I was clowning."

"Well then, I'm glad," she said, thumping the map with her forefinger. She looked at the mileage chart. "Because according to the map, Tacoma, State of Washington, is exactly 240 highway miles from Vancouver."

"Uh-oh. Facts. Now you're going to tell me Puget Sound blows things out to sea, right?"

"Which means"—she held up her hand, calming herself as much as him—"which means," she continued, softly now, "that when you talk about Bobby's molecules you're talking science fiction."

"We'll see."

She folded her arms. "I thought you said you were clowning."

What had upset her was Owen's reference to Bobby Fischer's close proximity. Within a matter of days or perhaps of weeks, he said (he wasn't clear on this point), Bobby's physical flotsam—she imagined, from images she had seen of him on TV, Fischer's shallow exhalations, his flaking skin, the errant hairs combed off his scalp, the clear Canadian air pushing his voice out into the world— that flotsam, the testaments to one's daily presence, would drift in attenuated form toward Tacoma and might on the microscopic or even cellular level mingle with the body of her husband.

What was she supposed to do with his statement? So Owen desired to be washed in another's debris. It seemed self-loathing somehow, not simply fanciful, and behind its whimsical surface she detected what she had in the past year come to acknowledge as his increasing remoteness. She pictured those cracks on Mount Rainier that ice-climbers were always talking about: the ragged lines were inviting as lips, but sometimes they opened with a roar and exposed a dark and giant chasm.

"Look," he said, closing his eyes, "would you get *off* it, already? I'm sorry I said anything."

"I just don't like it when you go on like that."

"Did I mention I was clowning?"

Did he even know what he actually thought? Or maybe she was at fault, reading too much into things, as he always claimed.

Really, who knew anymore?

Owen made a show of tapping his watch—he had to be at the Tacoma Chess Club by nine at the latest—then turned on his heel and grabbed the scuffed leather briefcase containing his chess paraphernalia (clock, board, chessmen, two pens, scoresheet booklet, M&Ms, aspirin, plastic coffee cup, spoon) and raised his hand on the way out the door. "See you," he said, not turning, and as he gingerly made his way down the steps, burdened with his clanking briefcase, his legs seemed to bow, and he rubbed the fingers of his free hand together vigorously, a sure sign he was still angry with her.

"Good luck," she called out, but she was dismayed at the pitch of her voice, higher and sharper than she had intended. She cleared her throat. From the back, he reminded her of a flightless bird, one of those giant storklike things she had seen in a high school text: a thin chest and wide, bony trunk; a balding dark head that in the morning light of summer—it was already steamy and bright, vaguely Asian in her estimation—looked wet in patches; wiry, firm legs and arms. There was something both heroic and ludicrous about Owen's purposefulness, a small, quick man on his way to play in a local chess tournament not even mentioned in the *News Tribune* despite Owen's repeated calls to the City Desk.

Maybe she shouldn't have mentioned the paper's omission as she paged through the Sunday edition, spooning in her breakfast grapefruit and watching him hunt for his aspirin. Maybe then he wouldn't have felt the need to start blustering about Bobby's molecules passing through him. And maybe she wouldn't have felt the need to plant her spoon like a flag into her grapefruit and rummage around the tool drawer for the *Texaco Road Atlas*. But the irony of what he was doing that morning was so apparent, so obvious, he must have been thinking the same thing as she: on June 2, 1971, at approximately 8:30 a.m., up in Vancouver, B.C., grandmaster Bobby Fischer was preparing to leave the Hilton to play in a world championship qualifying match discussed nightly on Walter Cronkite. At the same time, Owen Greef, employee-manager of the Big Bear Car Wash on South Tacoma Way, was preparing to leave his tiny house to play stinky fat men at the Greater Tacoma Open.

Her mother, Shirley, had phoned the night before. Shirley was in declining health but remained admirably vigorous in her opinions. "Are you watching this?" Shirley said. "Bobby Fischer on Channel 7?" There was a pause, and Bridget pictured her mother seated on the couch, unscrewing the cap to some bottle of bracing liquid the doctor had recommended. Bridget knew what was coming, and she could not help but agree: Bobby Fischer had the goods; Owen was simply embarrassing himself. Shirley coughed into the phone. "You could wipe your feet on him," she said, "and your shoe would go right through. There's a *world* out there, and the world expects things. Either you count or you don't." Bridget nodded. She swore she could smell her mother's medicine bubbling up through the receiver.

Bridget and Owen lived in the south part of Tacoma, at its farthest point, in unincorporated Pierce County, on a crumbling street where neighbors were set far apart, separated by mole mounds, patches of foxglove, and spindly firs that grew heavy with moisture and sometimes dropped sodden branches onto cars. Even after two years of marriage, Bridget was not sure how, in a legal sense, the unincorporated part of the city differed from the incorporated part. She knew only that the houses around them were dark and peeling, and that everyone's yard was treacherously soft, rotting underfoot from the seepage of decaying septic tanks. It rained a lot, and in the aftermath of storms or drizzles, gray still pools appeared on the swayback roofs and out in the rough terrain of the street, and everything got muddy and smelled like forest. Late into the evening, after the air turned chilly, insects walked the water, their pinprick ripples the only movement, and you got the sense you were not in Tacoma at all, but in some place ancient and recurring, one full of drainwater and holes, like a stretch of battleground.

"What would you think about moving?" she said to him last night, but he was having none of it. "Not now," he had answered, and she saw he didn't mean no, not this season, but literally not *now*: he was studying an opening, preparing to trick some opponent at the Greater Tacoma Open. He had highlighted some symbols in his opening book. The chess pieces on the board in front of him seemed to be placed every which way, without pattern. And now this. How dare him. His wild talk about cellular mingling, his denials: it was like sitting on a bus with someone who refused to drop a coin into the pay box. You weren't completely sure what was behind the act, but none of the possibilities was acceptable. It seemed to her outrageously unfair that she should be expected to read Owen correctly all the time. He was a child, he really was, and this obsession with chess was like a child's imaginary friend. What kind of friend? She'd like to know. Beast or confidant? Wearing a mask or not?

Once, early in their marriage, Owen had leaned close, drunk, and told her with much feeling it was hard to reconcile the two, chess and real life. They were like two cars roaring down the same freeway, and every once in a while the drivers glanced at each other with puzzled, longing looks on their faces and thought they recognized someone they knew. It seemed like something out of a sci-fi movie: space and time out of whack, two parallel universes keeping pace, each hinting of its existence to the other, each with something the other wanted. When she told Shirley what Owen had said, her mother had confronted her. Which car, Shirley asked, did she think he wanted to drive in? Look at the facts, dear, she said: look them right in the face. The facts, Bridget knew, were against her. Owen was the Tacoma Chess Club's rating leader and immediate past secretary of its advisory board. Most Thursday evenings he was away—he was the club's lock-up man four nights a month—and if you added in the occasional weekend tournament in Seattle or Ellensburg or Ocean Shores to the club's monthly weekender tournament, he was gone eight or nine evenings every month, with two or three overnighters.

But he was playing a *game* for God's sake, not going to cockfights or strip clubs or biker bars. Trust was not an issue, not in that sense. Always, he had been her little Odysseus, driving off to have his adventures, and he always came home. He was self-regulating. Dependable.

"You let him go out that much?" Shirley had said, alarmed. Lindsey, Bridget's friend since high school, didn't understand either. She had been calling for Owen's head from the beginning. "Who paid for his car?" she'd say. "How much of your paycheck went into it?" Lindsey had taken psychology courses at Tacoma Community College and wondered aloud if Owen had been autistic as a boy. At first Bridget laughed and told Shirley and Lindsey she was a chess widow, but she quickly stopped using the term because it suggested his time away was the issue, and because, as a title, it was so absurd she wasn't sure if her situation was actually worse, or better.

If someone had asked her in college what she thought about the game, she would have laughed. Chess was what geeky high school boys played, or cigar-puffing titans of industry. But now . . . she couldn't even mention Owen without picturing his roll-up vinyl board, the "tournament-ready" one with green and cream squares big as teacups. He did not put an alarm clock on the night stand. Instead, he rose for work at the car wash to the ticking of his wooden Jerger, his big lumbering chess clock with two round clock faces looming over their bed like the portholes of a tiny ship. Sometimes he pinched his fingers together for no reason at all, and though he denied it, she suspected he was playing chess in his mind and clutching imaginary pieces. Once, the two of them sloshing around in the tub, she swore she felt the weighted bottom of a pawn on her naked back, where his hand was caressing; when faced with the material evidence, he claimed, unconvincingly, that his fingers had somehow scooped up the piece when it fell from his pocket into the bathwater.

No, the issue wasn't how much he was away. The issue was how he always seemed to be elsewhere. There was a difference. Perhaps, she wondered sometimes, perhaps she was making too much of his—what?—hobby? love? life's work? The words seemed inadequate and off-center. There was no room any more in the world, in her world, in *their* world, for what he did. Owen and his chess friends had their own laws and hierarchies, their own silly wordplays—"check, mate," they'd say, calling over a waiter—and they clammed up tight about chess in the presence of those they called civilians, or people who didn't play.

She couldn't blame them. Even now, Shirley would stare at Owen across the dinner table with a look of horrible expectancy, as if sure he was about to rise and give form to her unease—the way, at work, Bridget could sometimes spot returning marines by their rabbity comments about Vietnamese. Well, there you go, Shirley had said. Your mom's right, Lindsey had chimed in: there's something obscene, something lurid about grown men piling into cars and driving long distances to play a board game from morning to night, for hours on end, just sitting and staring at chessmen until the only people out on the streets were cops or drunks. It brought to people's minds the perverse, narrow band at either end of a bell curve. It seemed close to sin, somehow: Thou shalt consort with others. Thou shalt not flee.

The house was quiet now as a monk's cell, so quiet Bridget could hear the air churn; it made a small roaring in her ears. She filled her coffee cup and watched the steam rise. Did she truly hate him? "He's my husband," she'd say in the early days, first to Lindsey, then to Shirley, and she'd throw her hands high into the air. But things were different now. Things hadn't been the same in ages.

Back then, during their first year—was it only a year ago?—he'd pull into the driveway at night, back from one of his weekend tournaments, and he'd be tired and sweaty and his mind would still be whirring, a sensation he compared to a car engine fan that wouldn't shut off even after you closed the garage door. Long before she began locking the doors around nine and curling up in bed with their dog, Alister, Bridget always had cold fried chicken waiting for him, Owen's favorite, and a nice macaroni salad with lots of sweet pickles and onions, and the trash would be emptied and the rug swept free of dog hair.

For a long time, she considered it important to make sure his returns were special. They'd eat with napkins instead of paper towels, and she took small, precise bites and made sure not to drop anything on the floor or swipe a finger across her plate to get at the mayonnaise and sodden chicken skin. They'd talk about her day, her long drive to Seattle to work, the proliferation of junk mail, Lindsey's new haircut, Shirley's latest doctor's report, and if the evening was clear they'd sit out on the patio and hold hands and look out into the darkening street, where distant trucks rumbled like surf and the pavement was straight and flat as a summer waterway. Sometimes they made love outside, discreetly and quietly, Owen taking care to cover them with a lawn-chair cushion, and sometimes they'd go inside and walk directly to bed and Owen would say, "Come here, come here, I want you to meet someone," and then she'd pull on the elastic band of his underwear and peer inside, and they'd roll around on the bed and squeal like children.

Lindsey said any dog could mate; all Owen's friskiness proved was he knew the difference between boys and girls. But that's not what her nights with Owen *felt* like, at least not at first. Every morning she dressed in uncomfortable pumps, a scratchy skirt, and a stiff, crinkling blouse and drove an hour up to Seattle to her job at Boeing, where she filled in complicated schedules and checked technical reports for administrative compliance. She made good money, but all those stuffed shirts! All the bickering, the need to be right every time, what she called the cult of competence. All the dreary cleverness. The busyness. Every day, she shuttled between warring factions working on Boeing's proposed Skyhawk modifications, scheduling bossy Army colonels who wanted four rocket launcher pods into meetings with smug flight engineers who favored wider killing zones for the existing two pods.

It was godless, headache-inducing work, and though she could not fathom now how she possibly could have felt this way, being with Owen had calmed her sense of dread about what she was doing with her life. Crazy. She even began to suggest—how could she have? it seemed impossible now—she had even brought up to Owen the possibility of her working more overtime, so he could cut back at the car wash and devote more time to chess.

That they had gotten married at all was a source of confusion to everyone. At first it had seemed sweetly impetuous, a madcap romance, and she loved his shyness and quiet, odd passion. The attraction was hard to explain, but professors at Smith sometimes married truck drivers, and GIs married minor Vietnamese royalty, and movie stars married horse trainers, so who was to say? All she knew was she had come home upset from the dentist on a Tuesday, and phoned him up, and started to cry. "I think we ought to get married," she said, her voice breaking.

She remembered feeling calm, even as she pawed at her tears, as if she were reading from a script typed out days in advance and slipped under the door. Disinterest, that's what it was, like an actor observing her own performance. Her mind seemed to be thinking in all directions, very clearly. Boil the carrots when you hang up. Call the optometrist. Remember this, *this*, for our children someday, for us, this sense of rightness. This airy grace. And she filed away, too, the mysterious connection between what she was now saying to Owen and what she had heard at the dentist's office. There, a white-smocked technician had told her that when archeologists examined excavated skulls, they always checked the teeth carefully, to help determine age: the more worn, the more *formerly there*—the technician's exact words—then the older the person at the time of death.

The idea had horrified her. There was an awful symmetry to finding a person's teeth worn down to the nub at the end of a long life. Body and spirit, both grinding down in perfect harmony into nothing, in cahoots with each other the whole time, grinding and grinding with exquisite timing, without error or deviation. That's why she and Owen were perfect. No symmetry. He was preposterous and uneven, and as they talked and cried and spoke softly into the mouthpiece to each other, she saw herself in the hall mirror and thrust out her arms and spread her hands wide, and everything about her posture—the taut line of her arms and hands, her arched back, the strain of her calf—spoke to her of the truth of her feeling.

Their first year, she sometimes accompanied him to tournaments. The playing halls seemed populated with the inhabitants of a fantastical island: swaying gluttons in overalls; smooth-faced, squeaking men who looked like women in suits; stumbling graybeards with piss stains the size of walnuts on their pants; stocky types with dark hairy arms and booming voices and a hacking, moist way of laughing; silent, staring college boys in brown lumberjack shirts who seemed to appear and disappear at will, like forest sprites; stumpy slow-walkers she suspected might have Down's syndrome; swearing, dull-eyed hoodlums whose faces were bright with acne. They all stared at her hungrily, and she felt their eyes roam her breasts and legs, and, once, in a crowded hotel elevator, someone briefly pushed his rolled-up plastic board up her skirt.

At the Rose Parade Open, down in Portland, she had sat by herself outside the playing area, inside the venerable old Oregon Hotel, which still attracted wedding parties because of its brass railings and ballroom and mossy blue carpeting. The hallway's high ceilings and chandeliers were in stark contrast to the other depressing venues she had been to previously. The grandeur of the hotel suggested serious conversation and old-world courtesy, and she wondered, briefly, wildly, if she would see players in suits or perhaps even evening wear, their ties tucked neatly into vests, black shoes gleaming. She sat reading a paperback mystery and sipping coffee from a Styrofoam cup, and the sun was shining outside, gliding in on dusty columns. She heard *Für Elise* piping through the hall, and, pressing her ear to the giant closed door of the tournament room, she could make out the muted noises of Round One: sharp, barking coughs; the occasional thump of a weighted piece landing hard on the board; an orderly clacking, like someone knitting, the sound of players making their moves and depressing the plungers on the chess clocks. There was an air of dignity and artistic endeavor about sitting in a comfortable chair, listening to small sounds that were instantly recognizable, like breaking a code, stripping away a barrier and suddenly understanding, suddenly seeing the logic of a thing. She put the book on her lap and smiled at the ancient desk clerk. Perhaps she had been ungenerous in her attitudes, unfair to Owen and his dreams.

"You waiting for a master?" a voice said. A tall man stood over her. He had wavy red hair and spoke with a silky bedroom baritone. He smelled of sweat and cigarettes, and a chess scoresheet was peeking out of his brown shirt pocket.

Then the door to the tournament hall burst open and at first she could not tell what she was seeing, something rapid and blind, a blur of arms and legs—players, she realized, young boys waving boards and rattling chess boxes, all of them open-mouthed, in cutoffs and T-shirts, shouting now, their faces distorted with laughter, jerking with quick, small steps past her and down the hall. "Oh Mama," said one of the boys, directing a frank, leering gaze toward her, and out of the corner of her eye she saw the lips of the tall man stretch into a hideous smile.

It was too much.

"No." She smiled up at the man. "Just waiting for the halt and the lame. Am I on time?"

The encounter had seemed funny at first, but then the truth of it—its hopelessness, its finality—depressed her so much she could not go to work the following Monday. She told Owen that from here on in, he would have to drive to tournaments by himself. It was a hard thing to do, to admit the strain she felt, and though she berated herself for her betrayal, she would not back down, even in the face of his pleading.

Desperate, she sneered at him over her scotch and water. "You're not so special, you know. You're not one in a million. You don't need a groupie."

His face turned hard. "You don't want to be with me, fine," he said, and he stood and left the room.

She had a trick for dealing with what Owen called her inadequacies, and she used it during her first weekend alone, when Owen was playing up in Renton. The trick was to find substitutes for the reasons behind her misfortunes, and imagine those substitute reasons were true. If, for example, she woke up half an hour late, she told herself she hadn't overslept because she had drunk herself into a stupor the night before, she had overslept because she had to stay up with a suicidal friend. If she didn't talk to coworkers, it wasn't because they didn't like her; it was because an administrator had assigned her to work alone, in a small cubicle. If she didn't raise her voice to her mother or to Lindsey, it wasn't because the very idea of shouting them down turned her insides syrupy and quaking; it was because she was kind and gentle and mindful of the needs of others.

Lately almost everything seemed a substitute for something else. If they didn't have breakfast together anymore, that was the same as Owen getting longer hours at the car wash. If they hadn't made love for over a month, that was the same as one of them lying unconscious in the hospital. If Owen said he wanted to be washed in Bobby Fischer's molecules, why that was like . . . She thought hard.

Here came Alister bounding in from the outside, through the dog door. Bridget was frowning. Her coffee was still warm. She raised the cup to her lips with both hands, as if it were a tremendous weight. Why, for Owen to say that out loud was the same as him stripping off his clothes and walking outside and standing in the middle of the street for all the world to punish.

Alister started barking, nudging her legs, but she laid her hand on his head and stilled him. She stared hard at the door, furrowing her brow like a mentalist. She stared a long time, narrowing her eyes, the way she had seen Owen look at his chess positions. She pursed her lips the way she had seen Owen purse his, bulging and tense, whenever he was looking for the saving move. For the miracle, he said. The move that puts you *in* the position. She couldn't hear herself breathe, she couldn't feel the chair, but at last she pictured the door opening. It would be hot outside, sticky as jungle, and she would have to squint to make out the shapes: car, sky, street, a crowd circling him, hooting. Owen, she would say. Her voice would be urgent and clear. She would walk to the street and hiss at the crowd, she would raise her arms and bring her fists crashing down upon them, she would make them cower and weep, and they would fall to the ground. You're here, Owen would say. Me and you. Here.

Anything
You Want,
Please

Six months after moving in together, Reuben Gill revealed to his fiancée Joanne that his application for Peace Corps had finally cleared. "Don't feel guilty," she said. Then she blew her nose and smiled at him beautifully. "You want this," she said. "Go. You've been waiting a year." He had, that was true. But there was no Joanne a year ago. He was head over heels, and when he handed her a tissue he started crying, and they held each other and rocked back and forth.

They lived in a boxy adobe house in Buckle, Arizona, where the smell of asphalt rose from the interstate at night and settled over the silverware and china. They had no money and no prospects, and the highway for miles each way was empty, but they loved the emptiness: every touch, every look had weight, and even from a distance their voices were clear and sharp. When Reuben showed Joanne his packet from the Peace Corps, she stood motionless by the front door so long he excused himself and went to the bathroom sink to wash up. She came to him then. Her hands were moist on his back. She said love was baroque. She said if she could, she'd step out of her skin for him and let the whole smelly mess

plop onto the floor. That's how baroque love should be. That's why
he should go.

So he did. At Subang International, in Malaysia, he phoned her
and covered the receiver with kisses when she answered. Later, when
speaking to the women in his Peace Corps training group, he re-
ferred to Madeline, then Kate, as Joanne. On the bus south, down
to Seremban for training, he talked to Hank and Reggie, and when
he said Joanne's name he saw his hands move, as if caressing. The
reflex startled him, but no one was paying much attention. Hank
told Reggie the air was heavy as a paw. Rounding a corner, the bus
narrowly missed a naked child urinating in an open sewer. Then a
lorry almost hit the bus, or seemed to: the Malay driver braked
hard and stopped inches from a ditch, kicking up dust. For miles,
the fruit trees along the road were spiky and red, and when Reuben
smelled them he was suddenly hungry.

In the second week, everyone bought hats with wide, floppy brims
and spoke with Australian accents during breakfast. Reuben, laughing hard, wondered what he was really doing. He bicycled up to
the Peace Corps training site, still wondering, and sat in the language classroom, saying *woo-woo* each time the Oxford-tie Malay
up front whacked the vowel chart. Hank and Reggie chanted along,
whispering jokes out the sides of their mouths to Kate and Madeline.
Reuben couldn't follow their banter. He was wondering what
section of his brain would be lit up if he had one of those synapse-
activity dyes the instructor had talked about. His mouth was making noises—*woo-woo, woo-woo*—but in some corner of his mind,
some insistent, demanding corner, he was asking how, last night,
he could have staggered past a woman sweeping rat pellets into a
pile and then fallen down drunk in a wicker chair, yelling "Whiskey, boy!" snapping his fingers, mouthing a stubby Thai cigar into
pulp. He wondered how he could have sat like that all night, queasy

with chloroquine, slapping at smoke-stunned geckos, singing dirty lyrics to "Oh Suzanna" with Chinese alcoholics, the whole bleary bunch of them an arm's length from a hacked-up sow dying in the doorway. Or how, earlier, at a roadside breakfast stall, he could have rubbed the chest hair of a fat Sikh ("Is lion hair," the Sikh said; "is good luck"), then let the man pretend to shave him with a tiny, pearled dagger, kitschy as a Monopoly marker, dangling from a keychain. How, he wondered, could he feel his body tremble with recklessness when his head was still buzzing with Joanne?

After class he walked to the trainee bunkhouse with Hank and Reggie. They were all frowning from the heat. Reuben's hair was stiff with sweat, and when he came in out of the sun and saw Geronimo Donaldson in the far corner, soaking his feet in a laundry tub of beer bottles and cold water, his scalp started to tingle. Geronimo was naked except for a dirty plaid sarong bunched loosely around his waist. He was the cultural orientation leader, an up-country volunteer who earned extra cash by showing newcomers around. Even now, sloshing his feet in the tub, he was unnerving. He had no body hair, his skin glistened like plastic, and he was always staring, bug-eyed behind thick hornrims with an elastic strap, what he called his oil baron look. His real name was George, but he said Oak Park, Illinois, had been so dull that simply leaping up from the dinner table made him yell *Geronimo*.

"Gentlemen," Geronimo said, grinning. "Everyone make their beds this morning?"

What Reuben saw folded on his pillow looked at first like a gift of cloth. It was yellowed and creased; it had a design. Then he understood: it was a newspaper. An article had been circled in red. The headline was "Amok Injures Estate Workers."

"Amok," said Reuben, tapping the paper.

"That's right," said Geronimo. "Same as English. To run amuck. They use the noun form here."

Reuben swayed a moment, alarmed, recalling his night at the bar, then his roadside shave from the Sikh. No one had seen him, not even Hank or Reggie. Hank, from New Jersey, always smelled like garlic, even after bathing, and his blubbery presence became obvious the minute he began wheezing or wiping his face with his shirt. Reggie was still jet-lagged and spent most of his spare time sleeping. He was bald and sweaty, with a dimple on the top of his head; he would have stuck out in a crowd like a balloon. As for Geronimo, he had been holed up in the conference room all week, arguing loudly with the program director about training procedures. Yet there was the article—*amok*, it said, *amok*—on his bunk.

"Rube, it's for you," said Geronimo, pointing to the paper.

Reuben felt the heat from his roommates' bodies. They were behind him, probably craning their necks forward to read the circled article. He imagined them breathing silently through their mouths, so as not to announce their snooping. They would feel bad for him: his behavior was being questioned. Perhaps he would be sent packing, put on a bus to Kuala Lumpur with a ticket back to Buckle in his pocket.

"Hey, not to worry," said Geronimo. He wagged his finger at Reuben, as if to say *I know what you're thinking*, then splashed water in his direction. "It's just titillation," he said. Then he leaned forward and spoke in a low voice. "Rube," he said, "paste it in your scrapbook."

No one made a sound. Geronimo just sat there, glistening, his lips drawn tight, eyes steely behind his hornrims. Hank and Reggie stood motionless by the door. The sun was so bright the jacaranda blooms outside had turned the color of chalk.

"Yeah, I can paste it in," Reuben said, lifting his head. He heard his voice quaver. "Sure. Just a sec."

From his travel bag he withdrew a pair of baby scissors—for his toenails, for pulling out splinters—and set to clipping. Splashing came from the tub. Geronimo lifted his feet from the water and ambled over, leaving wet tracks on the cement. His sarong was wrapped around his waist like a towel.

"Hombre," Geronimo said, pinching the scissors closed with his thumb and forefinger. Hank and Reggie still hung back, standing by the window slats, feigning interest in the insects smeared on the glass. Geronimo spoke softly so only Reuben could hear. "White boys in Buckle cut," he said, bending at the waist. He shook the scissors. "White boys in the bush *tear*."

"I know where I am," said Reuben.

"Yeah?" said Geronimo. "So tear, Rube. Titillate yourself. Get her out of your head for a change."

"What is this?" Reuben whispered. "What do you know about me?"

"Hey," Geronimo said. "I've been there. Personal experience, you know?" He tapped his head. "I can read your mind."

The words were astonishing, especially coming from Geronimo's mouth. This refugee from Oak Park, Illinois, this virtual stranger, a man perhaps with little loyalty to another life: this man had somehow grasped the problem in clear, if reductive, terms. Titillation as antidote. It was like snorting cocaine to stop smoking.

"Listen," Geronimo said. He put his mouth to Reuben's ear. "A little titillation, it's like giving her a vacation. From your head. You know what I mean? You don't have to evict her. Just let her out sometimes. Give her some air and clean your noggin up."

Reuben pictured his letters to Buckle. He had licked the stamps and rechecked the address. He had personally dropped them down the Out Of Country slot at the post office, safe from prying eyes. "Who told you this?" he said.

"No one," Geronimo whispered. "Come on now. You know you want to. Come on. Just tear. Just a little."

So Reuben tossed the scissors on the bed and placed his fingers at the bottom of the paper. He tore, straight up, ripping the paper cleanly, all the way to the article, then around. Geronimo cocked his head like a dog. Reuben leaned forward, listening. The newsprint was cheap; it made a sound like brush parting. The paper felt dusty in his hands, and the fibers dangled when he tore them, pulpy as tiny buds. Before he knew it, he had ripped a ragged hole out of the middle, and the hole framed the room like a window. He held the paper out stiffly and looked through the opening. He saw Geronimo rocking slightly, eyes closed, lips curled in, rubbing his fingers together hard, like mandibles, and by the door he saw Hank and Reggie, their faces pinched and alert, looking out across the trainee compound into the trees, as if they heard something rustling about.

Mail didn't catch up to the trainees until the third week. When Joanne's first letter came, Reuben set his face with an expression of brooding. He had never seen so much of her handwriting before. He traced his fingers over the words, then stuck the letter in his pocket and walked along the road, alone, sweltering, smelling the diesel drifting in from the logging trucks, and he became nostalgic and quiet. When he ate that night he thought of ice cream and chicken pot pie, and in the warm night air he swore he smelled spaghetti. The moment turned him weepy: Joanne's dinners were clouds of steam and pasta; the food made them drowsy and they slept without blankets on their big red couch.

That was her first letter. The second was covered with butterfly stamps. *To remind you of home,* the letter said, but Malaysia had more butterflies than he had ever seen in his life. There were so many, they made the field by his bunkhouse move, and when they flew, their wings left a fine dust in the air that settled on the plants. The letter made him teary—*miss you so much,* it said, *I say your name into my hand and hold you all day*—and so he stood in the field, mice scuttling underfoot, bicycle tires blistering against the gravel in the compound, and just looked at the butterflies. "Now that's titillatin'," he said to himself. "Titillates me to the bone." Later he napped on a palm frond big and cushy as a blanket. By an Indian temple the next day he put his nose to a crumbling wall. It smelled like chutney. He scraped it with his finger and a brick fell apart. Wedged in the mortar was a yellowed slip of paper filled with hearts and inky Chinese script; dark stains dyed the wall in patterns that looked like faces. He felt eyes on him. He stepped back and saw a naked Malay boy crouched like a cat by the entrance, resting on his forearms, just watching. He wondered if he were hallucinating.

Titillation: The restaurant bins were dumped in the sewers, and before the sun burned off the morning mist, the air in town was sweet and buttery as cornbread. In the afternoon, the heat soaked into his pores and pressed for hours like a hand, a woman's soft, insistent hand, against his skin. Some days he swore a tongue was licking his ear. The women wore tight polyester dresses; they thought he was exotic; they flirted outrageously. The old men doubled over with laughter when he sneezed, the stars were in the wrong place, and the spiders grew big as saucers and in his shoes they laid quivering eggsacs the texture of sponges. At night, the frogs' mating calls were so loud they seemed to be coming from his bunk. When everyone slept, he looked out the window and saw the silhouette of the palms lank against the night sky, and in his dreams the trees whispered to each other and made kissing noises, and sometimes they leaned through the bunkhouse window to touch him.

Some days he imagined himself as a bead of water on a griddle. He was jittery and feverish all the time, and he walked faster than he ever knew he could walk. After the rains, when steam rose from the fruit rinds heaped in the streets, he felt so light he had to cinch his belt for fear he would walk out of his pants. He looked into the outhouse mirror one day and couldn't believe the white face reflected back at him was really his. He put his fingers to his face. His skin felt hard and wet. His whiskers had stopped growing. It was a trade-off, he said. You feel a little strange when you learn things.

He learned, for example, that Geronimo followed him around. Once, walking past one of the outbuildings, Reuben yelled when something grabbed his arm; it was Geronimo, sneaking up from behind. "Don't bumble in the jungle, hombre," Geronimo whispered, shaking his head. Sometimes at night Reuben heard what he swore was Geronimo's motorcycle whining in the distance, but then he'd look up and see Geronimo peeling fruit, gobbling rambutans or lychees, staring at him. Or Reuben would be at the well taking a bucket bath, splashing cool water over his head, when he'd sense someone nearby. There would be Geronimo, naked except for his sarong, covered in leaves and tiny bits of wood.

"Don't you bathe?" said Reuben.

"Sure I do," said Geronimo, picking off a leaf. "The trails are bad here. Real dusty. This stuff sticks to you."

Geronimo told him a cross-cultural story that apparently no one else had heard. Reuben was flattered. He kept the story to himself until one night Madeline came into the bunkhouse, steaming. She called Geronimo a pig. He had leaned back against a tree, she said, and scratched himself immodestly, right in front of her, and when she brought it to his attention, he said, "That's the lesson. Just say what you want." Then he stopped scratching.

"I don't like being tested," Madeline said. "He's got no right."

"He gave me the Roseliana story," said Reuben.

Madeline had never heard it. "It's not so good," he said. "It's just a list, really." Madeline insisted. She wanted evidence that Geronimo had some sort of problem.

The story was Geronimo had taught in a tiny school up in Trengganu State, where he was in love with this Malay woman, Roseliana. She was the school secretary. She always looked at him coyly, face down, eyes up. Geronimo said all the Malay girls acted that way when they wanted to drive the white boys crazy; even his students did it to him when they handed in their papers. He walked into the office one day between classes and asked her if she could order some fluorescent lights for the boys' bathroom. There was no one around. She stood up and leaned against the wall. "Anything you want, please," she said. She looked at him. He stared a moment, then took her clipboard. "How about this?" he said. She said okay. He took the stapler off her desk, then a calendar off the wall. Okay.

He could see students milling around between the classrooms, but he took her watch off, then a barrette from her hair. She was doing pouty things with her lips, laughing. He took a pencil sticking out of her pocket. His heart was pounding. He opened a file drawer and took out personnel files, stacking them on her desk. He lifted a globe of the world and set it on the floor. It was all okay. He took out a slat from the window; he took a drink from her water glass, then threw the sponge for the mimeograph machine onto the floor. She moved around some, little motions with her fingers on the sides of her dress. She was smiling.

"Please don't tell me they went at it like rabbits," Madeline said.

"No," said Reuben. "The punchline's not very titillating. The ending was he couldn't figure out what to do next. He started thinking, If I go any further, there's no turning back. And he started wondering what exactly she meant by 'anything you want.' Maybe she just meant she would go order any equipment he wanted. Or maybe she wanted to do it, right there on the desk. Or maybe she was being passive, just going along with everything until he crossed a line. Maybe something else."

"So we learn that Malays are hard to read," said Madeline, folding her arms. "Gee. Impressive."

"Maybe," said Reuben. "He said the class bell went off and all these students came running in with lame excuses. Roseliana just stood there for a minute, kind of flustered, and then went back to business. Like it's no big deal, right? But he says he started thinking about what he could have done. All those possibilities. He couldn't get them out of his head. He could have just . . . I don't know. Done *anything*. You know what I mean?"

"I'll tell you what," said Madeline. "Around my neck of the woods, you don't get any damn thing you want. I got rules."

"Well, sure," said Reuben. "It's just, I guess I feel sorry for the guy." He pictured Geronimo telling the story. Geronimo had been leaning against the flagpole in the courtyard, drinking an Orange Crush, rolling the bottle across his belly. Geronimo said things got sour between him and Roseliana after that. He kept thinking about what he could have done, and it scared him. His voice sounded raspy. He stopped once and placed the mouth of the bottle over his left eye, then over his right, rotating the rim slowly, not pressing hard. His chin quivered a little. He was probably crying. He looked so lonely propped up against the flagpole in his filthy sarong, the sun behind him, gnats crawling on his face, that Reuben invited him in for a game of Othello.

Reuben wrote to Joanne about life in the bush. *Three months already!* his airgrams said. *The culture is much different. The men hold hands, and the women don't smoke.* The words seemed so empty he held his head in his hands and pressed it hard, the way he would press a melon in the supermarket, squeezing here, knocking there, and when he felt his fingers tap against bone he laid his head down gently on the table, imagining himself back in Buckle, moving on to another bin of fruit. He wrote her lots of letters. *When I get back, yeah baby,* he wrote. *Keep a candle burning. I got one burning for you.* He had a picture of her in his wallet. When he wrote, he laid the picture out on the bunk before he picked up a pen. The words came easier when he could see her, and when he rubbed his finger over her face he made sure not to press hard.

One night the program director played blindfold chess in the common room: no board or pieces, just calling out the moves. It was an amazing feat, beyond belief. Memory so clear and pure you could bring it alive, have it come pouring from your lips. The tips of your fingers felt it; you could touch a tiny chess piece and move the plastic to a square, and everything would be right where your mind said it was. It seemed heroic as love.

He asked her for more pictures, then a lock of hair. *Hair?* he wondered. He looked at the word his hand had just written. It seemed a reasonable request, not desperate, though when he thought later about what he had asked for, he felt a little foolish. On the way to language class, he bought a rambutan fruit. It was covered with wispy strands. He stroked them, then plucked a few off and tucked them into his shirt pocket. In class he heard Tuscany pirates had once held Malay princes for ransom. Suddenly his request made sense. He asked so many history questions Reggie jabbed him in the ribs. Ransom. His letter to Buckle was ransom: Give me things, and you'll live. A trade.

Nights, they all drank beer and prepared for practice teaching. The compound, a vacant boys' school, had a kitchen with a row of giant steel rice cauldrons, big enough to sleep in, and they did their lesson plans sitting in them, drinking Anchor, their bare feet sticking out. Reggie and Kate shared a cauldron one night, snuggling like teenagers on a carnival ride, rubbing their legs together. Everyone grew quiet, and after a while Reuben heard only breathing and his own lips sucking on the bottle.

"Madeline," said Reuben. He patted the sides of his cauldron in invitation. "Come simmer with me."

"Women aren't interchangeable," said Madeline, craning her neck forward. Her cauldron was at the end of the line, near the counter. All Reuben could see of her was her head and feet. She had painted her toenails red, and she jangled with bracelets when she walked.

"Hear, hear, Mr. Letter-A-Day," said Kate. "Someone cool him off."

Reuben wriggled in his cauldron. He put his hands on the rim and let his lesson plan book fall to the bottom. He got out of his cauldron so quickly it tipped over, clanging, then he walked down the line to where Madeline was. His face was red; he was breathing hard.

"I never said you were interchangeable," he said. "I got a fiancée."

"Just not here, huh?" said Madeline.

"Gotcha," said Hank. Only his head was visible; he was smoking clove cigarettes, and the sweet smoke rose like steam over something edible.

"All I said was 'simmer,'" Reuben said, eyeing Madeline's bare feet. "Just simmer, that's all." Her toes wriggled, as if in acknowl-edgment. He was suddenly afraid he might cry if he said more.

"Oh, come here, Rube," said Madeline, lightly. She patted the side of her cauldron and moved over, propping the lesson plan book over her shirt like a bedsheet. Reuben climbed in, careful not to touch her when he grabbed the rim to steady himself. Her pants leg was warm against his, and when they went back to filling in the blank pages of their lesson plan books, they wrote funny notes on each other's pages and let their bare arms touch.

In his letters, Reuben grew demanding. Send me your business card, give me your bracelet. Send me a tape of your voice. Give me the scent you wear.

She sent him everything he wanted, and more. The first time it was the button he had nibbled off her silk blouse. Then there was a mug, wrapped in tissue: the first cup they had both drunk from, the time she put cinnamon in the coffee. He could not recall when that was, and his failure to remember caused him such confusion he wrote her back immediately, talking about nothing, just happy to finish and write WITH LOVE in big block letters above his name. She wrote him back about her sex dreams and her crying fits. She filled a whole page with *I love you*, over and over, in big letters pasted onto the paper. The letters had been cut out of money. Each one, she said, was from a different ten-dollar bill. He didn't know what to think. "Guys, I shouldn't show this to you," he said. He showed it to Reggie and Hank anyway. They called him a five-hundred dollar stud. They gave him high-fives. "I'm just a cad," he said, but when he spoke his lips lingered over the word, and he said *cad* to himself in private just to feel his mouth say it.

"If you're a cad," said Reggie, "then let's get some poontang."

"Use it or lose it," said Hank. "Big Brother Peace Corps don't slap your wrist on Saturday night. I know a place in town."

"How do you know a place?" said Reuben.

"Geronimo," said Hank. "The man knows a certain house of ill repute."

"Some place," said Reuben.

"Coming or not?" said Hank.

Reuben shook his head. "Hey, I'll be there in spirit," he said. He watched them bicycle from the compound, down the dirt road. He could see their headlights move faster and faster the closer they got to town. "Don't let the bedbugs bite," he yelled, but when he saw Kate and Madeline staring, squatting by a tub of soaking clothes, he was ashamed, and he walked away.

Joanne sent him her diaphragm next. "Jesus," he said quietly, then turned around in his bunk so no one could see. He threw it in the trash. He told Reggie and Hank he had gotten moldy brownies. Then he got a tube of her red lipstick. At first he was alarmed, thinking it was blood: the tropical sun had melted the contents like a crayon. He laughed about it. He showed it to everyone, and when they laughed too, he laughed even harder. "*Ain't* that something?" he said. "*Ain't* it?" He threw the tube in the trash bin, and when he saw the next morning that dogs had knocked the bin over and carried the tube away, he wondered if he would see her diaphragm on the street some day. He couldn't imagine anything funnier. He laughed all through breakfast. He felt dangerous, and when Madeline and Kate bet him a beer, he drank hot onion curry straight from the bowl on the table.

Joanne's letters were so full of sex he was aroused when they arrived. But as he read them again later, his head swimming with beer, he was stirred not with arousal but with something else, something quiet and strange. He had the sense he was reading her words through two pairs of eyes: the pair that read and the pair that watched him read. The onion-skin paper seemed filled with hieroglyphics, with passion meant for someone else, for someone not even present, like a heart carved into a tree, containing names he didn't know. How? he asked. How can anyone live with such desire? Where can it go?

He sat at night in his bunk composing letters back, acknowledging to himself his own confusion. He sat stripped to the waist, the mosquitoes feeding at will; he nodded constantly, as if in agreement, and drank beer so quickly he got headaches. He told her nothing: his letters were full of anecdotes and turns of phrase he knew she would interpret as clumsy declarations of love. *Joanne, I saw the sun come up. Was it the same sun for you?* Or, *The women here are beautiful, okay, but so is chocolate cake. So are whiffle balls. It's not the same.* He wanted his other pair of eyes to see what he wrote. He would hold his letters up to the light. What his other eyes saw was deceit, and when he told himself he was writing deceit, when he said the words out loud, he felt light as a bubble, as if he would float to the ground if someone pushed him from an airplane.

When he received a pair of her panties, Reggie and Hank were standing over his shoulder watching him tear the package open. "Hey, hey," he said, holding the frilly silk aloft. "The letter's mine. Hands off." Reggie and Hank grabbed the panties, then threw them on his bunk, whooping. Were they new? he wondered. He left them there and went off for language class; when he came back the cleaning boy had straightened their bunks. His was empty, and when he checked under his bunk and in the small suitcase in the corner and found nothing there, he whistled in relief.

So the next Saturday night he bicycled into town with Reggie and Hank. They smoked dope in an alley, leaning against a wall that left their shirts brown and wet. They told vicious stories about everyone, then walked to the whorehouse. Its walls were covered with burlap sugar sacks. Inside the main room was a bead door, and when they pushed through, a Chinese man with a cyst on his neck leered at them questioningly and made an obscene gesture with his forefinger and hand. When he met his girl, Reuben spoke his desires harshly. He saw the look on her face; she thought he was joking. "So what you do?" he said then, imitating her speech. He felt himself scowling, as if he were sucking a lemon rind. "How much?" he said. He slapped his wallet against his palm. "How much you want? What you do?"

Reggie and Hank met him later in the hall. A table had been shoved against the wall, and the man with the cyst brought over beers. Reggie and Hank couldn't stop talking about their girls. They lined up their empties like a picket fence on the table. They were sweating hard, so they took off their shirts. The hallway smelled like a crawl space. "Ooh-*ee*, am I wasted," they said. Reuben looked at their nakedness. He was high and drunk, but he stood and called them liars. He knew what they were doing. He was sure of it. They were picturing themselves in Iowa and New Jersey, perhaps posing for a wedding photo, perhaps eating at a picnic, or crossing their legs in a crowded theater. They could feel the hands of their girlfriends warm in theirs; they could smell the stale skin of white-haired relatives, hear the affectionate words of their neighbors, touch the hair of small, trembly nieces. They sensed everyone nearby, somewhere just out of sight, and they were saying *I don't know you anymore.* They might as well have been plucking their eyes from the sockets.

Later, walking alone, staggering past the Cantonese drunks, Reuben saw a man sitting on a piece of cardboard, peeling a large spiky fruit. The man leaned against a giant, bulging sack, driving a spoon into the fruit to extract the pulp. When the fibers broke against the husk, Reuben heard the little tearing sounds, like stems being yanked from the ground. He held his arms out, as if to take the fibers in his hand, to roll them between his fingers, but he felt only the air, thick and warm with the exhaust from the diesels barreling past. The night was sticky and damp. When he woke in his bunk the next day his lips tasted of cloves and mud.

One day Madeline had a package for him. She walked into the men's bunkroom and smelled what they were smoking. "You can get kicked out for that shit, you know," she said, waving her hand like a fan.

"Smokes from Geronimo," Reuben said. "From the man's own hand. You going to say no to that?"

She looked at him with one eye shut and crinkled her nose. "Did you want the Peace Corps or the Marine Corps?" she said.

The men laughed. They aimed invisible guns at each other. Ker-*pow*, they said. Ker-*pow* and ker-*pow*. Reuben groaned as if wounded; he pushed back his chair and laid himself out on the cement floor. Hank staggered over to the beer tub and dumped the water out, then sprawled in the puddle. Reggie grabbed hold of the table and shook it. He brought his forehead down hard on the Formica top. "I am slain," he said.

"It's from Joanne," said Madeline, holding the package out.

"Reuben," said Reggie. "I'm serious. I think my head's bleeding."

"So bleed, already," said Reuben. Then: "The Marine Corps's it exactly, Madeline." He held out his arms and she threw him the package. He put it under his head as if it were a pillow.

"Reuben," Madeline said, looking him in the eye. Her lips were parted as if she wanted to say more, but she just folded her arms and walked out. Reuben watched her go. She was righter than she knew. He wanted to be a killer.

"Reuben," he whispered, in a high, faraway voice.

"Hey," said Hank. "I can do Madeline better than that." He said Reuben's name in falsetto. Hank said he could imitate her even better, and the two men rocked their heads back and forth and started saying Reuben's name over and over.

But it wasn't Madeline's voice Reuben had imitated. It was Joanne's. He whispered his name again, accenting the first syllable, the way Joanne spoke when she wanted his attention, and he put his finger to his head. He pulled an invisible trigger. He imagined Joanne sitting up in bed, yanking the sheets up over her knees. She would be wrapping a package with twine, stuffing—what? her breakfast? her bra?—into a box, nibbling at her long hair. She would whisper his name, and he would go ker-*pow*, ker-*pow*, ker-*pow* and she would see his clunky body laid out stiff on the floor.

Reuben kept packages and letters from Joanne in a cardboard box, grown soggy with water from the beer tub and the occasional rain. The box was stuffed with clothes on top, and when he received letters he read them, then plunged the paper through the shirts and pants like a white hot poker. The letters said *Reuben*, but now he could feel the pleading in the word. *Reuben, where are you?* the letters said. *Where are you, Ruby?* He had a whole boxful of pleading. He put a canvas backpack over the box, but still he heard it rustle at night with small, mewling sounds that disappeared only when he stared at it hard.

Later he gave packages from her to the cleaning boy. Most of the boy's teeth were missing, so when the boy smiled, Reuben saw his gums. He imagined the boy gnawing the packages open, wetting them first with his tongue, his hands shaking with excitement, his nose flat against the paper, sniffing.

Geronimo put his hands on Reuben's shoulders early one morning and began massaging. Reuben was seated on a bench, eating steamed noodles with his fingers. "Bro," Geronimo said, "how'd you like to see a real Peace Corps house?"

"Bro?" said Reuben. "Since when am I your bro?"

"Hey," said Geronimo, "you don't want, I won't say it."

Reuben shrugged. They left in the evening on Geronimo's motorcycle, veering past a convoy of logging trucks on the main road, then bounced down a dirt path near a fence post. The trail was patchy and full of snakeskins and scrub, and the leaves and dust blowing up from the tires stuck in their sweat, matting their arms with dirt and tiny sticks. They passed piles of rotting foliage in a clearing and, farther back, a circle of shacks on stilts, lit by lanterns. The road began again by a row of shophouses with tin roofs, then ended suddenly by a heap of sewer grates in a ravine. In a clearing, Reuben saw a lean-to. A lantern had been looped around a pole, and in the light he could see the ground was covered with lumber, as though walls had been torn down and laid flat in the dirt, like a sidewalk. A tiny Malay man in a Muslim skullcap rose from the darkness and waved. He was stirring a wok. Reuben heard a cleaver click against the metal. Against the tarp he saw the shadow of something long and thin, like a tail, and then the lean-to was gone, replaced by jungle, and the footpath grew so small Reuben thought of veins: tiny ropes burrowing into dense, fatty palms, the knuckly banyan roots underneath, a wall of bark and vines on either side.

Geronimo's house was nothing much: it had shuttered windows, and the planks were old and wormy. The stilts were missing in places. Piles of muddy bricks supported the floor.

"I thought this was going to take hours," said Reuben. "That's what I heard. 'Geronimo's place is *hours* away.'"

"You know how it is," said Geronimo. "All the scenery looks the same off the main road. People lose track of time. It's different for everyone."

Inside were tiny, stuffed red chairs and a wooden desk, the type used by Malaysian schoolchildren. A few watercolors of water buffalo had been taped onto the wall planks, along with a stained calendar advertising a tractor. "Kitchen, so-called, down there, bedroom over there, well and wash-up floor out back," said Geronimo, pointing. "Johnnie Walker cabinet here," he said, nodding at a chest of drawers in the corner. On top lay a cassette player that he stared at and thrummed his fingers on before pulling a lantern and a bottle of Johnnie Walker from the bottom drawer. He lit the lantern's paraffin wick.

"This is wonderful," said Reuben. "This is Peace Corps."

They sat down in the red chairs and drank the bottle from stained plastic cups rimmed with chew marks. Reuben thought he had never heard a man talk so much: Geronimo told him how the movie theaters were too cold, how The Beach of Passionate Love, up north, was full of chiggers and sand crabs, how in Bangkok you could ride elephants on the street and buy a girl for the price of American shampoo.

Reuben reached for his cup, but his aim was woozy, and he spilled the liquid onto the planks; he could see it collect in the cracks.

"No prob, bro," said Geronimo. "I got the best vacuum cleaner in town."

Reuben was drinking from the bottle cap when he heard Geronimo call him. "Out back, Rube. Come see the vacuum." Down the back steps was a cement floor surrounded by a wall of corrugated tin. Geronimo was standing by a stone well, turning a rope crank with both hands. It creaked; the rope was frayed, patched with something shiny and black, like tar. "Shh!" Geronimo said, and kept turning. Reuben peeked into the well. It was pitch black. The air smelled fetid, as if something were rotting in the water. Reuben stepped aside, crinkling his nose in disgust, suddenly aware of screeching in the air, a tight howl, and when he realized the sound was coming up through the well, he turned to warn Geronimo, who just shook his head. Reuben saw fingers clawing up the sides of the bucket. Geronimo held the crank with one hand and reached down into the well with the other, and his extended arm began to shake, as if something had grabbed hold.

"Hey!" Reuben said. He stepped back.

"Relax," said Geronimo. "It's the vacuum cleaner." He pulled his arm up, and holding onto his wrists was something tiny and thin, with a tail. It had a pruney, shrunken face. Its skull was round as a ball.

"It's a monkey, hombre," said Geronimo, smiling. "It's my little bro, Hoover." It opened its mouth wide and screeched at Reuben, baring its teeth, then used the top stone as leverage and held Geronimo loosely around the neck, like a baby. "I put Hoov in the well when I'm away," said Geronimo. "He likes to tear things up. He sleeps in the bucket when I'm gone."

"God, he stinks," said Reuben. The air was putrid and sweet.

"He takes some getting used to. But I'll tell you, Hoov's the one to call when there's a mess. He'll suck up anything your little heart desires."

Back in the living room, Geronimo threw Hoover to the floor. "This way, Hoov," he said. "There's some yum-yum for you." The monkey put its face to the floorplanks and stuck out a long tongue, lapping.

"*That*," said Geronimo, "is titillatin'. Huh, Rube?"

Reuben nodded. He couldn't keep his eyes off Hoover.

"Tunes?" said Geronimo. He handed the cassette player to Reuben, then bent over and stroked Hoover's head. Hoover looked up and chattered a little, then stuck its head into Geronimo's cup, lapping up more Johnnie Walker. "That's a good Hoov," said Geronimo. "Give big bro a kissum." He kissed the top of its head. "Oh, he's a hungry little guy. Did you hear that stomach? We gotta get Hoov some munchies."

A tape was already in the cassette player. Reuben pressed the Play button but was disappointed at what came out. It was a woman's voice, whispering. The tape was so scratchy he could hardly hear her over the roar in the background.

"So who is it?" Reuben said. "I could swear. . . . Who is it?"

"I don't know," said Geronimo. He was sitting cross-legged on the floor, holding Hoover in his lap, tipping the cup up to its tongue.

"Come on. Who?"

"It was a gift." He shrugged. "The cleaning boy. You know how he is."

"I know this voice," Reuben said. What he heard didn't seem to be music at all, just roaring and this woman's whispering, and when he looked up questioningly, his eyes roaming the house, he saw the shutters were closed, even though the evening was hot. Winged insects were struggling in through the cracks.

Geronimo stood, folding his arms. "You know it really?" he said. Hoover squatted by his side, eyes shining.

"Yeah," said Reuben. "Really." He frowned in concentration.

"Listen. Listen real close."

"I don't know," Reuben said. "It's like Joanne, almost." He felt light, as if his feet weren't touching the floor. He was dizzy, his breath shallow. He thought he heard her whispering his name, but the roaring in the background crackled so loud he couldn't be sure.

"You think? Maybe it's just a voice out of nowhere," said Geronimo. "Spooky stuff, you know? Like how I know what you're thinking. I mean, I can just get *in* there." He grunted. "You just got to make up your mind, that's all. What do you want? Really?"

"Is it her or not?"

"Which you want it to be?" Geronimo said. He opened his hand, then closed it.

Reuben held the cassette player out and watched the tape move from reel to reel. That whispering. What was she saying under the roaring? Her voice was breaking, as if she had the hiccups.

"Your wish is my command," said Geronimo. He squinted into the lamplight. A leaf was stuck to his cheek. Small twigs dangled from his shirt.

"Please," said Reuben.

"Hey, sorry," said Geronimo. "I'm just a jungle junkie, not a love broker." He bent down and let Hoover crawl up his shoulder. In the lamplight, Geronimo's face was half in shadow, and when he spoke his lips hardly moved. He stroked Hoover's tail, and the monkey closed its eyes and laced its fingers around the earpiece of Geronimo's glasses. It gnashed its tiny teeth. It grabbed hold of Geronimo's hair and put its mouth to his ear, chattering.

"I just . . . I'm hearing something," said Reuben, pressing the cassette player to his ear. "I got to know what."

"All right then," said Geronimo. "All right. Now we're getting somewhere. Just put the tape player down. Right on the desk. Don't give it to me. Just put it down. Right there, put it down. Nice and slow."

Reuben felt his body tingle, and he saw his hand holding the cassette player, caressing the plastic window lightly with his thumb. Hoover began to screech and bare his teeth, and when Reuben tried to raise his arms to shield his face, Hoover lunged forward, for him or for the tape he couldn't tell, and Reuben's limbs just flopped at his sides. He felt Geronimo's hand on his. He looked down and saw the man's fingers around his wrist, guiding his hand to the desk. Together, they put the cassette player down. Geronimo ejected the tape. Reuben felt Geronimo's arm around his waist, moving him toward the door, helping him down the steps. He saw a flashlight beam illuminate the ground. He saw his body move, his feet step over roots, his hands pull aside brush. He felt himself walk awhile, staying inside the beam, and sometimes he caught glimpses of Geronimo at his side, holding Hoover's hand. He had no idea how far they walked. He knew only when they stopped, they stood in a clearing. There were thousands of flecks in the air, fuzzy as static, suspended in the flashlight beam. Reuben saw Hoover run into the beam, opening and closing his hand and stuffing his fingers into his mouth. Flying ants, Geronimo said. They swarmed this time of year. Hoover loved to gobble them. Reuben felt the tickly wings on his hands, his mouth, his eyes; he felt a blizzard of wings. They sounded like whispering. He ran forward into the swarm, straining to hear, but Hoover leaped up and straddled his neck and started to screech and screech and wouldn't stop.

Proof

Willy wondered how far he should go with Annie before he realized that *could go* would make things a lot simpler. They were in the Sears photo booth holding crinkled bags between their knees. Outside the booth, Willy's wife, Vicky, egged them on: "Keep your clothes on, now. Smooch, smooch." Annie was mostly her friend, though Willy admitted to liking Annie too. In truth, she made his heart race.

Earlier, at Annie's, Vicky had played around with their names. Willy and Vicky. Vicky and Annie. Willy and Annie. Willy, Vicky, and Annie. The sound was always *eeee*. Vicky stretched her mouth wide to say it, prompting Willy to raise his eyebrows: "What are you, a siren?" Then Annie stretched her mouth wide. *Eeee*, she said, smiling at Vicky, and together they climbed the scale, rising in unison from the couch the higher they climbed. They walked over to Willy, who was sunk deep in an armchair, and stood inches from his face, their mouths wide. *Eeee*.

"I yell like that when I hit the surf," Willy said. "God, I *love* exhilaration."

"Snow job," said Vicky.

She always said that. At home, she called him yin-yangy: he gaveth and tooketh away, all in the same breath. Steamroller, he would call her; then he would lie on the floor. But mostly they watched TV, shushing each other all evening.

"Think so?" he said to Vicky.

He looked at Annie, then back at his wife. "Well," he said to Vicky, "how's that for exhilarating?" His voice quavered, but when he heard himself he was not embarrassed. He pictured the pebbly beach at Alki Point, the Seattle skyline in the distance, gray as a mountain range, and he saw himself shirtless, smacking hard into the surf, yelling.

Vicky looked at him calmly. "Saying isn't doing," she said. She folded her arms in challenge.

"Hey," said Annie. "Hey."

But she didn't mind.

So they drove down to Sears, where Willy could give Vicky proof. Willy clutched the steering wheel so hard his fingers turned white, and Annie and Vicky drowned out the engine with shouting and laughing. First, all three sat in the photo booth, holding in their hands a paper bag on which the date and time had been scrawled in big letters.

Vicky and Annie went in next. "She's *my* girlfriend," Vicky said. "Wait your turn."

Then Willy and Annie went in.

Willy kissed her on the cheek in time for the first photo flash. "Oh, you'll like *this* one," Willy shouted out to Vicky. He imagined his wife staring at the curtain, fretting. She joked, but her cheerleading didn't fool him. He could hear the worry in her voice.

He lingered near Annie's face after the second flash. She smelled like oranges. Her dress looked silky, even in the darkness.

Annie turned to him. "*Eeee*," she whispered.

He kissed her on the lips, just as the third flash popped. His heart raced so hard he put his hand on his chest to slow it down. He felt powerful. He felt like a man who had just run into the ocean.

When Willy showed his photo strip, the three of them were silent at first, as though deciphering a telegram. Annie said she couldn't believe she was being so naughty.

Willy smiled at Vicky. "The proof's in the pudding, huh?"

Vicky smiled back, then showed her strips to Willy. Each picture was nearly identical. The women's eyes were closed. Their mouths were cupped together in deep kisses, their hands on each other's body.

Willy looked at the strip for a long time, registering what he saw. "You look like fish," he said, stalling.

"Looks more like octopus to me, lover," said Vicky.

"No, I mean your expressions," he said.

"What's that fish called?" said Vicky. "Is it a *grouper*? Or is it a *groper*?"

Willy pretended not to hear. He took the strip from Vicky and traced his wife's miniature face as though trying to recall her species. Her hair seemed different. Her cheekbones looked too high, her neck too long.

"That's my man," said Vicky to Annie. "Deaf, dumb, and blind."

Annie poked Willy in the sides. "Come on, now," she said. Her voice was giddy.

Willy looked at Vicky. "What's happening?" he said.

"What's happening?" Willy said again.

"You ought to know," said Vicky. "One word says it all." She put her arm around Annie's waist. "*Eeee!*" Vicky screamed.

Then Annie joined in.

The sound was so loud the floor help in Appliances turned their heads.

Willy stepped back. "Stop saying that," he said. His breath came in labored gasps; he felt cold. "What are you doing?" he said softly. He held his arms out in supplication, but when he saw that the women looked only at each other, he dropped his arms to his sides.

The women raised their voices.

Willy tried to speak. His mouth was so dry he could only clear his throat. He wanted to tell them to quiet down. But their voices filled the store, every aisle and carton, and then everything seemed far away, everything seemed somebody else's, like when you first enter the water.

Leo, Chained

Leo Culler, Malaysia-phile, was confident of distinguishing shit from shinola, though he freely acknowledged not being sure exactly what shinola was, only that it was not shit and had come, a generation back, in flat, round cans. He did not have asthma. What he had . . . he didn't know what he had, but it wasn't asthma. It was 1981, and he was thirty-eight and enormous and in bad health. That much was true. But he could still lift gigantic loads—a refrigerator once, sometimes a gross of cooking oil in ten-gallon jugs—and set them gently into the UN van. He could still stand on the dock of the Kuala Trengganu River, clipboard in hand, and just by glaring, safeguard oozing wicker baskets of UN cabbage—refugee supplies— from malingering Chinese thugs and Malay motorcycle cowboys.

No, he did not have asthma. Asthmatics smelled of paper. They had a hole in their squeezebox—*nee-nah, nee-nah* when they wheezed—and they took short walks in comfortable shoes. What, wondered Leo, would bag-of-bones Captain Richards have called his condition? Certainly not asthma. Captain Richards of the Scotsguards would have known, which was not to say anyone would have listened. Back in Peace Corps—back then! Leo marveled, back six years ago, back a lifetime—back then the Captain had been a blotchy old alcoholic who always seemed to be on his fourth Guinness. Most likely he was dead now. But back then the Captain drank at the Peace Corps bar and didn't mind all the Yanks going on about their bowels. During The Emergency in the '50s, he had fought Malaysian communists. Even now, with Vietnamese boat people swarming the east coast of Malaysia, fleeing their own communists, even now, Leo could hear the Captain grinding the gears of his Austin, roaring down Highway 4 and braking hard at some hairpin turn to point out the window.

"There," the Captain would say. "*There* was where we took fire, November of '54. Bloody Chinese." The Captain had incomprehensible grudges against his homeland—he never vacationed in Durrey, he had a loveless marriage to a Malaysian woman—and whenever possible, he let you know where you stood. When the Captain let you know, the words turned his eyes steely and bright. When he let you know, you saw he hadn't always been lonely and dying, that he had been vigorous once, his eyes clear, his desires sure and bountiful. You knew he hadn't always sat out back, among the pong-pong trees and jasmine, sucking on bottles of stout.

One evening, the Captain let a tourist know. The man was giddy, an Australian judging from all his winking, and full of ridiculous stories. "Incredible, hey?" the tourist kept saying. "Incredible, hey?" Captain Richards, who had been stiffening with each passing minute, inching forward in his chair until he was almost off the seat, slammed down his bottle and straightened. "You," he said. His lips were quivering. Then he let the tourist know. He pointed with a shaking hand at the fool, sweeping some bottles away with his other hand, as if to clear a pathway to the man, and said if you wanted to float down the bloody river, you better know that truth was hard as a stone and would bloody well send your arse to the bottom. The room went silent. Captain Richards's eyes welled up for a moment. His lips parted as if to say more, and his Adam's apple began bobbing, but then he leaned back in his chair, slowly, as if air were escaping, and when his back was again touching the foam cushion, he cradled his bottle to his belly, stroking the label gently, with his fingertips, the way a father strokes a baby.

Who would deny, wondered Leo, that such a man had known things to break your heart? Leo, wondering, sat at his desk. For the past ten months, an image of dying old Captain Richards had been nudging its way from the back of Leo's mind to the front. The reason seemed clear enough. For the past ten months, he had been with the UN, with the High Commission for Refugees, stuck in the city of Kuala Trengganu. He was staff liaison. He had a window facing the South China Sea. Every day he looked out the window and rested his head on his desk, despairing, wishing he was still with the Peace Corps. Had he truly given up his Peace Corps life for this? Six glorious years for more money and a title? The UN refugee business, Kuala Trengganu-style, stank.

Every month the boats from Vietnam arrived, packed with ethnic Chinese and Saigon shopkeepers and psychotic former ARVN Ranger Scouts. Thousands of them. In December the waves were roaring, and no one in town would buy lungfish or blue-striped angelgills because the bodies of drowned Vietnamese floated on the feeding grounds. The boat people sailed toward the Dutch oil-rig lights. The lucky ones skirted the coral and sailed all the way to the camp on Bidong Island, and Bidong Island was out there, just beyond his line of vision, a speedboat ride down the Kuala Trengganu River and out the harbor, past the seawall, thirty kilometers into the ocean. *Out there.* That was where he belonged. Not in Kuala Trengganu. Out where sweat meant something. Out where truth was hard as a stone.

But when he looked out his window at the lacy waves, all he could say was, "I need to be out there." He could not bring himself to press a finger to the pane and say Out there, truth was hard as a stone. The words were fierce and unforgiving. He thought of that woman, the seamstress from Quang Tri Province, a beetle-nut chewer who had waved a green lightbulb over her head, and, screaming *Grenade,* chased off a boatload of Thai pirates. He thought of the trawler manned by Thai monks, a ship laden with crackers and barrels of water, cruising the coastline in monsoon storms, scanning the waves with searchlights. He thought of the man—what was his name? Vu?—the man who later died in the Bidong Island hospital, the man with the blistering lips: he had squatted for weeks in a foundering boat and rocked his wife, telling her over and over her face was more beautiful than water.

Some things weren't yours to say. Some things, all you could do was rise in your chair and plant your fist on the desk. Those boat people: where they came from, there was so much blood in the soil the plants grew enormous roots; the stains on the walls made patterns resembling faces. When Saigon fell in 1975 the war washed into the ocean, out past the shoals of Xuan Tuan harbor and into the South China Sea, and now it tugged at the hulls of small wooden boats and seeped through the planks and licked at the ears of its children. Leo could feel it sometimes in the water where the fishermen dropped their nets, something hot and soft. When he pulled his hand out, his fingers were covered with tiny red bumps, as if touched by jellyfish. He could smell it on that awful beach up the Trengganu coast, where cheap colored sandals came in with the tide, dozens in the span of an hour, so many the villagers swore the sand crabs they ate for snacks tasted like rubber. And then the wood washed up, then the bits of cloth and plastic, the broken watches, the clots of hair stuck in shells. The war was out there, out where he couldn't see it, out there in the water, and it was pulling its children to its side, it was grabbing their arms and holding them under and whispering into their ears, *breathe me, breathe me.*

That was the truth, and it was hard as a stone, but he couldn't say it. Not with paper on his desk. Not with the phone-bill disputes, the astounding per diems, the air-conditioning drying his face. So Leo wrote on a roll of butcher paper what Captain Richards had said, and taped it to his desk.

"*Your* arse isn't getting to Bidong any faster," Ed said, folding his arms. "Not with poster-talk."

Leo tapped the sign with his finger and went back to work.

No one in the office thought highly of his sign. Out in the hall, Leo heard Ed call him a corndog. Leo bounded up from his desk and placed an immense hand on Ed's shoulders. Ed, he said, if you haven't floated down the river, stay home. Ed smiled. Leo punched him lightly on the shoulder. Ed smiled again. Leo punched him a little harder on the shoulder, and when Ed said Easy big fella, Leo said if he cared to stick around, he would show him just how unforgiving the river could be. Ed stuck his hands in his pants, then took them out and tucked in his shirt. He looked up at Leo with flaring nostrils and in a breathy voice said he had to go.

Leo's fist was curled. The veins in his neck pulsed. He stood growling, watching Ed retreat. He felt a whooshing against his skin, a hot wind urging him on. He felt the whooshing ripple past, he heard the papers down the hall rustle. But he did nothing. He just stood in the hall, shaking a little, doing nothing.

And then he had his first attack. He was flat on the floor by the time the secretaries heard him gasping. Asthma, everyone said, but they didn't know shit from shinola.

Leo said he sat in his chair a lot because the white man's burden was too heavy to carry. In fact, the humidity in Kuala Trengganu was killing. Everyone had been sitting in their chairs a lot lately, depleted and sleepy, but only Leo looked like a man about to expire. The irony was not lost on the staff: Leo Culler, Mr. Peace Corps himself, had worked in Malaysian swamps for six years. After six years as a Peace Corps volunteer, people said, you'd think he would have grown used to the heat, despite his lumbering size, his doorway stoop, his special-order Big Man Belts from Singapore. Excuse me very much, Leo said, but never had he felt air sticky as candy. Never had he known a whole city in need of a bucket bath.

Touchy, people said.

He didn't disagree. In his office, wiping down his chair, breathing as through a hose, he felt himself quietly seep through his pores, rising in small gasps through the office ceiling, clinging absurdly to curry fumes and the scent of frangipani.

The east coast of Malaysia was well into the monsoon season, but the city of Kuala Trengganu had yet to see a hard rain, even though November had already come and gone and the Kuala Trengganu soccer club had disbanded for the year. The puzzling thing was that the December rains had always fallen like clockwork, once in the morning and again in the afternoon. In normal times, just when Leo thought about loosening another button on his shirt, a hard rain would fall straight down in a sheet, as if from a carpenter's plumb line. The sheet would be bloated and warm, but it sucked the moisture from the air, and for hours the smell of earthworms would drift from the elephant palm and hang over his plate of noodles.

Now he couldn't ride in a trishaw without sticking to the seat. The streets steamed all day, as if someone had plunked him into a cauldron and shut the lid. Leo felt the moisture on his neck, and when he looked to the east, toward the South China Sea, he saw the mountainous clouds and hoped for rain. But when anything fell in Kuala Trengganu, it was wispy as hair. Still, every morning the market women wiped their faces with bright polyester scarves and held out their hands to feel for the first drops. Here it comes, one would say, and for a moment everyone would start chattering, rubbing their fingers together expectantly. Usually nothing happened. A plastic bag would stick to some woman's foot and remind her of warm water in a field. Sometimes a drizzle fell. Then the market umbrellas shimmered with dew, but in the end there were just miserly puddles on the asphalt and smelly warm steam clouds rising from the fruit rinds. Rubber sandals were still slick to the touch. Matches still wouldn't light.

The poorer sections of town were said to have turned dangerous. Once, Leo walked by the houses behind the worksheds of corrugated tin, just off the docks, and saw rocks raining from the sky. The air smelled like an old well, and out of frustration young men threw stones high overhead, as if to punch holes into the clouds. They said the walls of their houses had turned to cardboard, moist to the touch; the slightest breeze from the harbor felt like the hot panting of a dog. Farther on down the dock, Leo pressed his ear to the moorings and heard the water suck like mud against the boats. The washerwomen told him the air was so thick it was turning the stone of the access ramp soft. They squatted all day on the platform above the mouth of the river, dragging sopping dresses from their plastic tubs. They said they knew water well enough to know there was too much in the air, and when they dunked their arms in the brown river current and ran their fingers through the foam, sniffing and spitting, even as the sweat dripped off their faces, they bawled to each other that the lichen was growing so fast it smelled sweet as babies. Leo, rocking, checked under the moorings. Coconut husks drifted by in pairs, placid as sleepers. The river quivered with fish. It was thick and glistening, and when he wiggled his hand in the water he thought of cream.

Cream. Like a tourist would think. Like an old man. A hog. He broke a chopstick and pressed the jagged ends to his head.

Mornings, he awoke from dreams in a sheen of sweat and rose like a man climbing from a pool, eyes blinking, one hand placed high on his nightstand, hefting his considerable weight from the mattress. His body left a wet outline on the sheets, and after plucking drowned mosquitoes from his matted hair, he filled the room with Malay curses that floated out the window slats and into the curious ears of children trudging off to school. If he still had someone to write letters home to, he would have written that such humidity was not possible. But he had no one to write to back home, not after nearly seven years of watching letters from home turn into airgrams and the airgrams turn into postcards and the postcards turn into nothing. What he had were little white lawyers and immigration spooks in the UN office, and they did enough writing home to last everyone a lifetime. He saw their outpourings in the office mailbag, hefty envelopes bearing butterfly stamps, page upon page describing the growing languor they sensed among the weather-weary residents of Kuala Trengganu.

The anecdote told most often, related first by Ed from Nevada at the weekly office luncheon, was of the two city ambulances that wailed one night down Bungaraya Road, bearing old people complaining of dew in their lungs. Ed said he had prayed. He had seen lights click on in the stilted wood houses along the road, and dressed only in a sarong and flip-flops, he joined the families standing on their steps and expressed his sympathy.

Ed was informed by one of the Malay secretaries that the December second issue of *Berita Harian* contained a short piece about the weather. He bought a copy. The secretaries were right. The conditions in Kuala Trengganu, said the article, were driving away tourists. The head of the national meteorological society was quoted as calling the weather unseasonable, the result of high air fronts produced by the recent volcanic eruption in the Philippines. The sultan of the state said it was like a cup of tea that never grew cold.

"Typical," said Ed. "Not a word about Bidong Island. Can you imagine how hot the refugees must be?" Ed made it his business to be on the docks when the relief workers from the island came in on leave. He quizzed them on everything: when his six months in Malaysia were up, he was going to write a book of poetry about his experiences. He had heard the winds on Bidong came in from the northwest; small, inhospitable abutments, prickly with staghorn and madras thorn, closed off circulation to the camp as surely as a hundred foot wall. Ed wrote down *madras thorn* in his poetry journal. Once he saw a boat in the breakwater, far to the east, and was told it was Vietnamese. Refugees were on board. Sometimes they sailed all the way into the harbor. Ed whistled and waved, and, later, when the boat capsized, he wept bitter tears.

"Those poor Vietnamese," said Francine from Minneapolis. "And we take air-conditioning for granted. It makes you think."

"Question," said Ed. "If you could somehow bring air-conditioning to Bidong, would you give up your own air conditioner?"

"Of course," said Margaret from a small town near Chicago.

"Okay," said Ed. "Question with amendment. How about if the air-conditioning were only in the Malay Task Force barracks on Bidong? Then would you do it?"

"That's a much more difficult decision," said Francine. "I hear the Vietnamese do get to go inside the barracks, but still . . . Task Force. They're *guards*, aren't they? They're like prison screws everywhere. They're brutes."

"Question with two amendments," said Ed. "How about if the air-conditioning were only in the Malay Task Force barracks, and it was only on at night and the early morning?"

"Then I think I'd have to ask for numbers," said Francine. "How many Task Force guards use it versus how many refugees. I'd have to think about the ratio."

Margaret interrupted. "I bet I know who would rather give it to Task Force than the refugees," she said. She pointed with her chin, Malay-style, to Leo Culler's office.

"I bet you're right," said Ed. "But I bet you'd have to break his arm to make him give up air-con for anyone."

Leo was at that moment clenching and unclenching his fists in his office. He leaned against the door, as if to prevent his guest from leaving. "I mean it," said Leo. "If I don't get a transfer, I'm going to kill someone. It's just talk, talk, talk around here. All those yaps wide open and noise coming out. I need Bidong. I deserve it. You know it."

"As our staff liaison," said Doctor Johansson, "murder would reflect badly on your record." Doctor Johansson was the head of the Kuala Trengganu UNHCR office, in charge of all local mainland UN operations. He put his finger to his nose in acknowledgment of his joke.

"I'm not kidding," said Leo, slapping his hand on his desk. "These people are driving me nuts. Talk, talk, talk. Ed in particular. Margaret and Francine, too. All three. They're all on my list."

"Well," said Doctor Johansson. "I'd just turn the air-con on high. This humidity is driving me nuts too. You have to be patient. No guarantees, but maybe next time around your transfer will come through."

"Next time around is eight months," said Leo.

"I'm well aware," said the Doctor.

"Yes, of course," said Leo. "You're only head of UN ops here. You only hobnob with the prime minister. You can't possibly use any influence with the Malaysians."

The Doctor sighed. "And now the personal attacks begin," he said. "Let me tell you something my mother once told me. When I was a kid, I got in fights all the time. I gave the neighbor kids bloody noses. Now my mother, she pulled me inside by the hair one day, and she said something I've never forgotten. I know your inclinations very well, Leo, and I'm guessing you're going to laugh at this. But keep in mind this was directed at a ten-year-old boy. Keep in mind the spirit in which it was said. She hauled me aside and put me on her knee and she said 'Niceness is a thank-you away from goodness.' Now go ahead and laugh if you want. It sounds stupid, doesn't it? But it's really not. It's the golden rule. I think you'd do well to remember it."

"What do you know?" said Leo. "What?"

"That's enough," said Doctor Johansson. "Watch your tone."

"Come on," said Leo. "You talk like I'm all hairy balls and no brains. A two-hundred-and-sixty-pound stinkpot. I'm not. I can't help how I was born. You know my..." He wouldn't say it. The Doctor would just snort.

"Your title?" said the Doctor. "Yes. The Biggest White Man in Kuala Trengganu."

"So what? I won't apologize for it. I've got nothing to be ashamed of." He gathered breath. His lungs felt fibrous, his throat sore. He continued. "Talk, talk, talk," he said. "All these yaps going off in my face. It's too much. You're not exempt. You're on my list, too."

"Look at you," said the Doctor. "You're sweating. You look terrible. Are you having trouble breathing too? You are, aren't you? I'm not saying I agree with Ed, but isn't it possible that you, shall we say, drive yourself a bit too hard after-hours? Think about it seriously a moment, will you? There's no air-con on Bidong, you know."

"This again!" said Leo. "We're not talking about air-conditioning. Come on. We're talking about *doing* something. Snap, crackle, pop! Getting your hands dirty."

"Yes," said the Doctor. "Kicking some ass, right? The Biggest White Man in Kuala Trengganu storming Bidong and setting things right."

Leo opened the door and, with sweat running down his nose, stood stiffly with his hand on the doorknob, hoping to reduce the visit from the Doctor to a tableau: two men frozen, quiet as granite, their hair waving in the rattling gusts of the air conditioner. The Doctor would have to make a move, and the only place to move was out the door. It was clear the Doctor had no intention of pushing the Malaysians. The Doctor only talked. Everywhere, yaps were opening. There was palaver by the copier out in the hall, palaver drifting by from the receptionist's desk. Talk. Then more talk.

The Doctor brushed at some imaginary speck on his pants and rose, his smile uncertain. He hurried out the door. Leo pulled out a stubby black Thai cigar. But even now, when no one would dare enter without knocking, he found himself looking around. To his right were bound copies of UNHCR history, arranged on the bookshelf by task—UNHCR *Joins Hands*, UNHCR *Jumps In*, and so on. To his left was a mesh bag of donated soccer balls, ready for shipment to Bidong. He was alone, so he began to smoke. He ignored the degradation: a grown man sneaking puffs. But private degradation was infinitely preferable to hearing people say *Aha!*, then watching them run to report what they had seen. They would say his asthma was his own fault. Asthma! No, it wasn't asthma. He knew it wasn't. What, then? He didn't know. But he knew if people saw him smoke, they would run to the Doctor and say Leo Culler was acting irresponsibly and making his asthma worse. His asthma—asthma! Anyone could see it was much, much worse than asthma could ever be—his asthma, they would say, was brought on by his adolescent behavior: all that smoking and drinking, the late hours at Cowboy Lim's, where the hostesses dusted their legs with talc. And surely, *surely* if he needed to be on Bidong as badly as he said, he wouldn't be in such a hurry to ruin his health. Why, Bidong didn't even have air-conditioning. Sending him to Bidong might even be a death sentence.

If they knew shit from shinola, which they didn't, but if they did, they would know that he had to smoke and drink and keep late hours with disreputable Chinese hostesses. Why, he wasn't sure. He knew only that when he wasn't smoking or drinking or keeping late hours, his lifelong stuffy nose became something lurid and hysterical. His symptoms were frightening. He would pound his chest and gasp, taste salt on his lips, roll his bleary eyes heavenward. Oxygen trickled in as if through a straw. Sometimes there was nothing, just open-mouthed suffocation. In the aftermath, his face glistened, and a Peace Corps doctor, dropping in one day for a visit, had medically certified the blockage in his esophagus and given him a prescription.

From the staff he expected no understanding. They viewed the symptoms as self-inflicted, the body dishing out punishment for the abuses heaped upon it by its owner. So he carried around an inhaler, grasping it in his hand like a rock, and made sure everyone saw him carrying it around. Under the circumstances, carrying around an inhaler made sense. It was largely a psychological ploy— it said *See? I'm taking care of myself.* It made everyone think he was acting sensibly. If people thought he was acting sensibly, then maybe they would stop blaming him for his condition and start blaming his condition on Kuala Trengganu. Maybe they would start listening seriously to his request for a transfer to Bidong. Maybe, if he could just make them listen, they would reward him. But how humiliating the terms! How many bottles of Anchor, how many hostess legs, how many hours at Cowboy Lim's: how many it took to let him look himself in the mirror.

No one, including the Doctor, doubted Leo's physical discomfort. But Leo's resistance to its logical explanation simply confirmed what everyone sensed: that he was, in addition to his other faults, a blowhard and a liar. He was not, in the popular view, the kind of man Bidong needed, even if he were well enough to live there. Every chance they got, the staff emphasized the need for team players. The Doctor didn't think he was a team player, though the man was too weaselly to say it to his face. The little white lawyers and immigration spooks at least said things to his face, though when they said them they thought they were speaking in a way he couldn't understand. Francine from Minneapolis told him once if he went to Bidong, she would be glad to give him her supply of salt tablets. This humidity, she said. Without air-con, it would drive an *ox* to its knees. Margaret snickered. By "ox," Leo knew, Francine meant him. He knew she was speaking in a way she thought Margaret would understand, but not him. He knew she thought he lived in a sweaty, brutish world, and that when he suffered, he suffered extravagantly in the way of sweaty, brutish animals.

The argument of the little white lawyers and immigration spooks rested on certain irrefutable facts. His arms and face were chalky, mottled with nicks and freckles. The Malays said his skin looked like dog belly. Ed from Nevada had been with him when he started a set of Malay twins crying just walking past. Child eater, they said to their mother. Too, he knew everyone thought his outfits churlish. He favored flip-flops, severe dark T-shirts tight against his muscles, and belts with big, garish buckles. His nose was beaked and broken, uncertain in direction, like a leg on an antique table. He had what Margaret thought a buttocky way of eating. His mouth hovered over the food, lips smacking, and he kept wiping his chin with his fingers. In the sun, he would fix you with his stare as if in disgust, and his sleepy, hooded eyes narrowed to slits.

So every morning he walked into the office and saw in their eyes

a formal charge: You are not simply immense, you are engorged.
You are aberrant in the manner of typhoons and famine. Every
morning he wiped the sweat from his face and talked to little white
lawyers and immigration spooks who thought him a blowhard and
a liar. Not that anyone denied his wealth of knowledge. He knew
Malay, and he knew the people who spoke it, and his knowledge
was why he was staff liaison and jawed with the Malaysian Task
Force office. Where's the best place to eat? the staff asked. What do
you call a Malay witch doctor? Why do the men grow their finger-
nails long on their pinkies? When they call you *orang puteh*—white
person—to your face, is the term meant to be rude? Leo's answers
were fine—"Thank you! Thank you very much, Leo!" they said—
but each morning he felt their eyes roam over him, evaluating,
assigning equal parts pity and contempt.

Then there was that other fact. His six years with the Peace Corps
had done something to him. He couldn't shake it. Up in Kelantan
State, he had slogged through mucky swamps with a mosquito
fogger, handing out pamphlets on hygiene. Peace Corps, he would
tell anyone who cared to listen, had been baroque and ejaculatory.
In flip-flops and Japanese sunglasses, he spent six years bitching
about the Chinese to the Malays and bitching about the Malays to
the Chinese. He had killed a pit viper and strung its head from his
belt. Knee-deep in swamp muck, he smoked Kools with Malay boys
sleepy with opium; evenings, he drank beer with Chinese men who
scratched at lazy scars stitched down their bellies. He laid traps by
mangrove trees, capturing bulbous frogs the Chinese dried for rem-
edies. He had frothing, doggy sex with village girls atop giant sacks
of flip-flops. The fruits he ate had tickly spikes and smelled like
blood.

At first everyone smiled and said, "Well well," but within weeks
their faces betrayed nausea: their mouths screwed into grimaces,
they scowled, their hands went reflexively to their stomachs. He
understood. They had drawn a line, and they did not want him to
cross it. He gave them a feeling of contamination. Sitting at his

desk, he imagined what they must be whispering. Leo Culler: he's one of those damn heat, damn natives guys, isn't he? From a man like him, a man who would tell you whorehouse etiquette ("Etiquette! That's what he said!"), this guy who *claimed* he sucker punched a Thai kickboxer, this guy who loved his beer just a little too much—from him, hi and goodbye was as much contact as you wanted.

He heard them talking by the entrance.

"Six years playing Tarzan," Francine from Minneapolis said. "Is this what happens to you?"

He listened to her explanation then went back to his office and looked at himself in the glass of the broken copier. Yes, he thought, gazing at the reflection. That's what playing Tarzan does to you, and so what? At least Francine had been accurate in her explanation. His life did indeed have, as she put it, puerile appeal. It inclined toward cliché. His friends were barflies, and he had a roustabout's fascination with posturing: tough talk, a wicked tongue, an exaggerated sense of his own roguishness. Such a man, Francine said, was a surface skimmer.

She had a point, but after a few beers at Cowboy Lim's, he modified her observation to a pointlet.

If now, six years and ten months later, he was only a pig snuffling after truffles—Francine had muttered the words when she saw him standing by the door—then it was only because for years he had had more truffles thrust into his face than he could possibly snuffle in one sitting. Peace Corps had been hallucinatory as the heaven of Islam. In the swamps, cradling his mosquito fogger in his lap, he had seen the pink eyes of rats staring down from the rafters of his house. When he moved, the jungle paths moved with him, alive with leeches inching toward his veins. People squatted in the road, smoking pipes and spitting, posed as if in defecation. The old Malay women had skin tough as hides, but were limber as garden hoses: they could bat wicker balls high in the air with their feet, agile as major-league shortstops. The tropical heat was a tongue in his ear, licking all day, and he sweltered so much he swore hands were pressed to his body. Chinese men in singlets spat on the floor and laughed like jackals. All of it was arousing. After a rain, the slick tires piled in the streets smelled like hothouse sex. So did the food. Some days he was blue flame. In dreams he walked around with his body turned smelly-side out. He couldn't even breathe without thinking of the odor of open-heart surgery or food rotting in a pail.

It had all been so simple. He had a lean-to in the jungle. His needs were basic. Once, he had worked out a list of the one hundred words he would need to know to fulfill his needs. The rest was gratuitous grunting. The list was something of a revelation. With one hundred words you could eat, sleep, screw, and take the bus.

There were secret moments as well, moments for which the biggest dictionary was insufficient. He remembered nights dragging a box of empty Johnnie Walkers from under the bed. He sang, tapping the glass like a xylophonist, with the handle of a machete. He played the Stones and Creedence, and stared out the window at the sea hibiscus and elephant palm. The leaves shimmered in the dark, and then the whirring began. There were the small cries of prey, the rustle of hunting rodents. He would sit in a bubble of lamplight, his hands huge in the shadow, a bowl of noodles warm at his side, and a great *whoosh* would rise from his chest, like a wind, and sometimes his fingers tightened around the handle and sent the machete down hard against a bottle. There would be a sharp noise, a hard thunk against the floorboards, and then silence. Just like that, no longer than it takes to snap a finger, the banyan swamp would fall quiet as a forest of mushrooms. Outside, the plants and trees stopped whirring, like mechanical contrivances clicking off. His chest swayed to the pumping of his heart. His arms twitched, and he felt his lips swell with blood. Then he heard it: a clicking from somewhere inside his body, cartilage rubbing together, tiny bones speaking, knocking like a chick against its shell. As if something were trying to come out. As if something were inside him. It was the most wonderful sound he had ever heard. He wept in joy some nights, it was so wonderful. He ran to the door and kicked it open and yelled *Kiss me* into the darkness, because if he didn't yell *Kiss me* he would be alone in the jungle with the rats scrabbling across his roof and the leeches inching up the lean-to steps, and his spirit would float up through the holes in the tarp when he slept and he would awaken puny and oppressed.

"Kiss me," he would shout, opening his arms and stumbling down the steps. "Oh yeah. Come on." He said *Kiss me* into the elephant palm, and something did.

Some mornings he taught the words to boys and girls in filthy swamp villages. Their faces lit up in pleasure. Kiss me, the boys said. Kiss me, the girls said. They chased each other around sewer grates heaped in a pile. They laughed and nudged each other, but Leo knew what they were thinking. They stared at this giant white stranger and imagined in the lank palms around them the cavern-ous avenues of New York, where the movies at the Lido Cinema showed frothy love on every street corner, under the buzz of air-planes, in screeching taxis and blizzards of confetti. The words weren't words. They were magic. You said *Kiss me* and something did, only it wasn't really a kiss, it was something like a kiss, some-thing fleeting and sudden, something that made you think of a bird flying over the ocean. Sky above, water below. Just flying. Some-thing so beautiful you dropped to your knees, and when you dropped to your knees because it was so beautiful, all you saw was just some raggedy-ass bird flying over the water. Like a kiss. Just some greasy lips until they touched you. And when they touched you, when they touched you . . .

On buses he said the words into the ears of giggly Chinese chicken farmers. No one could hear over the engine. It made no difference. He shouted it out the rattling window. The bound chick-ens pecked at his feet, boxes rattled in the aisle. *Kiss me.* He was so aroused he had to place his travel bag on his lap.

But he knew some things sounded strange when you said them out loud to people. What the jungle meant—well, some things burrowed into your bones and wouldn't fit on your tongue no matter how much you called them out. Some things scared you, they burrowed so deep. Some things you couldn't say because they wouldn't let you say them. So when the little white lawyers and immigration spooks asked about his Peace Corps days in Malaysia, he didn't say It kissed me. Instead, he paused a moment and said, "The beaches are straight out of a movie," or "You want some real Chinese food, go to the Ooi Boong Suey." It wasn't a lie, but in his mind's eye, he saw himself spreading his arms and saying It kissed me. He saw himself saying It kissed me so hard it won't let go.

The little white lawyers and immigration spooks wouldn't understand. For one thing, the State Department rotated them out every six months, just when they were getting up the nerve to go out and order a roadside breakfast. For another, they had come to do good. Refugees! The UN! The moral imperative! For them, doing good was an extension of services already rendered. He knew the type: hugely educated children of the upper-middle class, on the fast track to both heaven and Georgetown. They had been on the track for years, all the way through college and tepid missionary-position affairs and into grad school and now Malaysia. For the boat people, goddamnit! That's what they said: We're here to help, aren't you? They had a pile of forms on their desks to back up what they said. In their cooing speech was the certainty of a script: those poor people, those poor Vietnamese.

Leo was not impressed. In the air-conditioned confines of the Kuala Trengganu UN office, what did such words mean in the regions of sinew and heart, cunt and cock? It was just talk. You opened your mouth and sat in a chair with your hands in your pockets. What did all that yappy high-mindedness mean to people foundering in the South China Sea, squabbling over the water jug? Those people, when Thai pirates pulled alongside, those people heard the gunwale-tires squeal, scraping wet wood. It was a sound like trumpets, and then pirate demons swarmed the deck, waving parangs. Those people, they had to put their underthings in a pile, where demons rubbed the folds for thin taels of gold. Those people got their ring fingers hacked away. They didn't care what you had to say. They cared what you could do.

Around noon each day Leo began to glower and clench his fist, conveying, he hoped, a willful brutishness, for only through menace, through the promise of fantastical, storied, physical harm, could he stop the staff from asking him to lunch. They did lots of smiling at the waiters and praised the food loudly, then hunched over their plates and shrieked at their cross-cultural foibles. Ed from Nevada said he'd been practicing his Malay all week, but instead of saying Where is the National Monument, he said Where is the National *flea*. Margaret from a small town near Chicago said the first time she heard the morning call to prayer she thought someone was playing the *radio*. Over ice cream they shook their heads knowingly at the stories about Bidong Island. Francine from Minneapolis said she heard the Vietnamese had stabbed a Malay Task Force guard, and then Task Force beat the guy who did it and landed him in the hospital.

Ed said, "Well, my appetite's gone."

Margaret said, "Those animals. Does the Malaysian military get their training in the U.S.? Is the State Department part of the solution or part of the problem? I'm going to bring this up in D.C. I'll bring it up. I will."

Their conversation was a sign of a more fundamental problem. People were, after a certain age, obliged to know shit from shinola—else they were obliged to throw up their hands and say, out loud, that their place was out back, among the pong-pong trees and jasmine. No one at the UN office would throw up their hands and say it. Ed told stories about how wacky he was. He was insanely patient with the Malay secretaries. On vacations he flew to Bangkok or Manila and came back with showy traditional shirts and a terrific tan. Francine and Margaret bought tiny dogs and left outrageous tips at restaurants. On weekends they took local buses just to see where they went, then wrote with such passion in their travel diaries they would meet for drinks and read them to each other. The three of them hated the banks because no one queued up, but they liked the Kuala Trengganu Coffeeshop because the sound system played traditional Malay music instead of Freddy Fender. They held baffling opinions. Taxis were better than trishaws because trishaws were too colonial. Johnnie Walker was worse than gin and tonic because it was too American. The police would deport you for being too frank about sex.

In the office they squinted when the locals walked down the hall. Malays, Chinese, Indians: when they were wearing western clothes, how could you be sure who you were talking to? They all had straight dark hair, they could walk all day without sweating, and they had the waistlines of schoolchildren. Leo wondered if the staff saw how touristy they were. He brought the subject to their attention.

"Oh please," said Ed.

"Please, please, please," said Francine. She put her hands over her ears in mock disgust.

But late one night, they all went down to the Kuala Trengganu Coffeeshop and had a few Anchors. They said they wanted to pick his brain. Brass tacks time, Ed called it. Francine said she had been doing some thinking. She leaned forward and said the Malaysians' skin color was misleading. She looked over at Leo. "Are you happy now?" she said. "So sue me. We haven't lived in this place all our lives."

What confused her was that the Chinese who worked outdoors could be dark as the Malays who worked indoors, and the Malays who worked outdoors could be dark as the Indians. Furthermore, the Indians weren't always black as coal—I mean, excuse me, said Francine, but black really *is* the color, isn't it?—and when you threw in the mocha-colored Indian Sikhs, you needed a scorecard just to order chapati. Okay, she said, that last part was uncalled for, just forget I said it. One thing, though: to know who was who, you had to see—really *see*, said Francine, see, as opposed to look at—

certain distinctions. The Chinese had flat, scrunched-in faces, while the Malays had heads round as beachballs. The Indians looked like skinny white people, except they were black and had even more nose cartilage, and when they talked they sometimes wagged their heads. The Malays looked kind of sulky and passive-aggressive, and the Chinese were always scowling, like they wanted to drive a stake through your heart. If you still weren't sure, you had to look at their hair: the Chinese favored brutal cuts, and the Indians always put on lots of goo. The Malays were always combing theirs.

"Are you children?" Leo asked. "Yes or no?"

Later they all walked to Ed's apartment, overlooking the botanical gardens. The Irish Creme was passed around, then the brandy. The BBC was turned off. What do you think? they asked Leo: up close, you have to be a little discreet, yes? The Indians and the Malays smelled like curry, so if you said you had a cold you could sniff them on the sly. The Chinese were easier. They gave off waves of medicinal herbs and sometimes reeked of ointments that dried on their faces like molasses. The Malays grunted to show agreement and had goiters and bristly, solitary hairs growing out of moles on their arms. But whatever you did, you had to keep in mind that the whole country was paranoid because of how the British had lorded it over them, so you couldn't stare or sniff too long. The exception was when you were in a restaurant, where everyone— Malay, Chinese, and Indian—just stared off into space for hours, like they were sitting for portraits. The Chinese, of course, had the best food because it wasn't like the Chinese food back home. The Indians had the most exotic fare because it came on banana leaves and you got to eat with your hands. The Malays ate Muslim food in filthy little shops and washed up in fingerbowls, which was a lot to ask just for food, so you might as well eat Indian or Chinese.

Leo stood.

"Where are you going?" said Ed.

Leo stumbled against the door. He clutched his throat. "Cowboy Lim's. I don't know. Jesus. This air . . ."

"Hey, no one's smoking in *here*," said Margaret.

"Stop it!" said Leo. "Enough. You people. I can't breathe." He heard voices rise when he shut the door. They sounded like tea-kettles.

In the office the next day, his stomach suddenly churned. His lips turned salty, his breath shallow and panting. He moaned, then leaped from his chair and ran down the hallway, massaging his chest. He opened his mouth wide, gulping like a fish. He ran past Ed's desk, then Margaret's. He doubled over next to the rubber plant. He opened his mouth and sucked. There was no air.

Later, he walked back up the hall, weaving a bit, holding a vial of camphor oil under his nose. In his office, he pulled out a black Thai cigar and lit up. The room was so quiet he heard himself wheeze. It had been a bad attack. His chest still hurt. He was jumpy. He fiddled with the air flaps on his wall unit, then opened his door just a little and stared out.

There was the rattle of the secretaries' desk fan, the dull-witted clacking of their typewriter keys. The two women, Fanizah and Zira, sat in the hallway, typing away every day with Islamic modesty, in rayon headscarfs. They had been with the Kuala Trengganu office four years. Every day they presented the same ridiculous sight. They stuck their heads out, craning their necks like chickens, whenever the fan propped on the coffee table sent a gust of wind their way. They were miserable in the heat, complaining loudly of headaches and tiredness. But even when he threw the door to his office wide open and cranked up his wall unit to high, the machine just made a horrible racket and sent forth black hairs that eventually inched their way across the blue floor tile into the path of the fan, which then blew them into the women's faces.

Had it come to this? A running war with little white lawyers and immigration spooks? Secretaries rubbernecking to the fan? Kiss me, he thought. Kiss me. Something kiss me or I'll die.

He waited until the secretaries left for lunch, then ran out and bought iced drinks in plastic bags, cinched with a rubber band and topped with a straw, Malaysian style. When they returned, stopping to wipe their feet at the entrance, giggling, he held the drinks up to their faces. They smiled. *Terima kasih*, they said. Thank you. He felt Fanizah's hand brush against his arm, and when he looked down and saw her look shyly up, he felt his stomach twitter.

"For you," he said, watching her drink.

"Yes-*lah*," she said, and began giggling at Zira. "I am drinking. So delicious." She held up the bag of liquid and shook it in his face. He smiled broadly and started to speak, but the women pushed past him and sat down. Leo watched them go, then walked back to his office. He listened. He could hear the women rustling. In the distance, Ed asked where the paper clips were. A phone rang somewhere. The photocopier in the hall was humming. He looked out into the hall. Fanizah and Zira were sitting at their desks, slowly guiding their fingers across their typewriter keys. The keys began clacking. The plastic bags of drinks were empty, heaped in Fanizah's wastebasket. And then Fanizah and Zira began craning their necks, following the movement of the table fan. Francine was marching up to Doctor Johansson's office. Ed was blowing dust off a ream of paper. The electric table fan went slowly back and forth. No, it was saying, turning to the left. No, and then it moved to the right. No. No.

So he leaped from his chair and ran out the entrance, pushing past Ed, who raised a paper clip in greeting. He clopped to the street. Cars. A fat woman with lentils. A curry zone. Tar and durian fruit. Bleating. Diesel exhaust, like wreaths. Something scratched his leg. And then grass, a cigarette pack collapsing beneath his sandals. He had no idea how far he ran. He knew only that he had run, and that he was now at the Kuala Trengganu dock. A boat was being loaded. A Malay man in a skipper's hat yelled through a bullhorn at two Chinese longshoremen. Leo's stomach was queasy. He praised the sweat soaking through his shirt, his uncombed, mushrooming hair, the vague tightness at the back of his skull. He was itchy and hot; the air was moist as a hand. Between the cracks in the dock he saw flatfish sway in the current. The longshoremen moved imperceptibly, staring at cases of processed chicken still stacked on the dock. The man in the skipper's hat sat outside the wheelhouse, scraping out an engine case with a screwdriver. The moment seemed to hang in the air. It had lost its forward motion, and in raising his arm to point at a teetering crate, in feeling the coarse threads of the shirt rub against his skin, Leo had a delicious sensation of watching himself move his own body.

And then everyone simply stopped working. "Vietnam," one of the longshoremen said. He clucked at Leo. "Vietnam boat coming." The longshoremen squatted and pointed to the east, toward the breakwater at the mouth of the harbor, where the river ran into the South China Sea. One of them passed around cigarettes. The man in the skipper hat stared, leaning against a giant sack of flip-flops. Leo looked. On the horizon he saw a boat ride the rough breakwater. It was so far away. From the dock, it looked like a splinter of wood. Leo shielded his eyes, squinting into the glare, trying to see. He felt heavy, and the longer he looked across the water the heavier he felt. There was nothing anyone could do. The breakwater was white. He thought he saw the boat tilt. He thought he saw it going down. He listened, but heard nothing. The longshoremen pointed. They moved their lips, but he couldn't hear them. He couldn't hear the moorings creak, he couldn't hear the seagulls overhead, he couldn't hear a sound. "Asthma," he barked, kicking off his shoes. The way he said it made the longshoremen jump. "Asthma," he sneered now, stripping. He said the word only to dismiss it, and when it scattered in the air—a cloud of phlegm and dust, a smelly damp powder—he leaped. He leaped because he knew, in every vein of his body he knew, he knew his lungs would carry him. He knew because something kissed him hard on the mouth and said *breathe me*, and he did, and now he was thrashing toward the boat, wrestling the current, swearing, now he was swimming an impossible distance through the water.

The
Big
Gift

The best news Owen Greef had heard all year was that Bobby
Fischer would be flying to Iceland to play for the world chess championship. Bobby versus the Russian, Boris Spassky. Bobby the bad
boy genius. What Bobby could do in a game of chess was what
Mozart did with musical instruments, what Michelangelo did with
brushes and paint. The whole country was in love with him, and
he didn't even care he was loved, or why.

Since his divorce Owen had lived in the Commodore Apartments, just blocks from the Big Bear Car Wash, where he'd once
been the manager. From his window he had a view of the gas tanks
and faded tar-lined roofs of downtown. Below him were bars and
secondhand shops and mysterious brick storefronts with boarded
windows. Mornings, men slumped against the peeling doorways
and talked about girls upstate who'd smoke you in broad daylight,
right in your car. At night the empty streets echoed with shouts—a
block away or six blocks away, it was so cavernous you couldn't
really tell—and newsprint scudded across the pavement and blew
rattling into your face.

It was astonishing to Owen that he now lived in the district. Facts were facts, but he didn't have to resign himself to them. No way I'm staying here, he'd say. Just no way. The Commodore stank of ammonia, and the orange-capped fat man who came over once a month to tend the rhododendrons and drag a push broom across the linoleum never bothered to toss empties into the Dumpster. Down the hall a neighbor had posted a sign:

Call Hospital if you make Noise.

Because I will Kick your ass.

When Owen first heard the news about Bobby—at Sears one afternoon the screens on all the demo TV consoles crackled to life, revealing row upon row of revolving chessboards—he stuck his hands into his leather jacket, and in a show of surprise and happiness pounded his fists together. He hadn't known. Hadn't been keeping up since his wife left. Beside him, a crew-cut salesclerk, stopping for the broadcast, began shadowboxing the space over a sale lamp. "Go Bobby," the clerk said to the TV screens. This was shocking. The clerk looked the football and baseball type. Then other people stopped, too. Two boys in dirty jeans. A black man in a green suit.

Owen sensed then a charge of energy in the air, a slowing of time, like diving into a pool, leaving one element and entering another. A pink-cheeked man holding a pipe wrench caught his eye and winked, as if in confirmation. Then a doughy blond in a miniskirt folded her arms and unexpectedly hoisted herself up onto a console, sitting pretty. Overhead, the fluorescent lights began to buzz, bathing the whole length of Console and TV in a humming soft light. On the TV screens, something he believed he'd never see in a public place: dozens of the same powerful hand shoving dozens of the same gleaming chess piece resolutely forward. The crowd stood as if hypnotized. It was a wonderful sensation, sensing something he'd buried come alive again, and as he walked out, late for his Yellow Taxi shift, Owen couldn't help but notice the air had turned rich with a delicious metallic-tinged perfume.

Around nine, a greasy teenager in a T-shirt leaned forward menacingly from the back seat. "Take Seventh Avenue," the kid said. "Seventh, man. That meter goes over eight bucks, I ain't paying. Nuh-uh." Owen let the challenge pass. He was summoning an image, straining to keep it intact. Queen pawn up, king knight out, other pawn up, pawn again, queen knight out, bishop out. Then what? The pattern kept dissolving.

"You looking to score weed?" said the boy.

Owen considered. "Don't smoke," he lied. Rolled tight in his jeans pocket were the remnants of a dime bag—he smoked Colombian Gold and Thai stick, popped white capsules stored in a peppermint tin—but there was insinuation in the boy's voice. *I got your number.* Owen had been pegged like this a hundred times. Meter jumpers, trash girls going off to get pawed, recruits bawling their heads off outside the gates of the air force base, sullen old Filipinos counting out exact change: they were all so far down they wanted to pull you down with them. Not this time. Owen, replaying his lie in his mind, made an inspired vow to keep his head clear. Maybe he'd given up on tournaments too quickly, after all. He was only thirty-four.

Even in the dark you could tell Owen's skin was still ruddy, and though he was losing his hair, what remained rode his skull in tight waves. In his teens he had practiced an expression, and the look had never left him. His eyebrows were dramatic and arched, his nose hawkish, and he had a habit of tilting his head down, just slightly, so that his big, dark eyes seemed to glower when he concentrated. They glowered now and all through his shift, and even after he signed off his taxi and marched straight from the garage up the Fourteenth Street hill, six rolling blocks.

The chess club was housed in an ancient storefront, set back into a concrete lot between apartments where all the women had bruises on their legs. There was a large picture pane window to the left of the door, and when Owen looked through he saw the familiar straight-backed wooden chairs and long wooden tables, each laden with boards and chessmen. He was in time. A game was still going. At the end of the back table, Wes Jackson played a shag-haired boy.

"If it isn't Owen Greef," said Jackson, turning at the sound of the door. Jackson was fleshy and wide mouthed, and when he spoke his tongue seemed to loll, spit-flecked and gray, like an aquarium slug. "Long time. I heard you quit."

"You heard wrong." Owen shrugged. "You playing much?"

"Here and there. My lady says I can't spend weekends on chess anymore."

Owen nodded sympathetically.

"Where you working these days?"

Owen shook his head. "Not the car wash, if that's what you're asking. You hear about Fischer?"

"Are you kidding? Who hasn't? You ought to start coming by again. Everyone's got Fischer fever now. We must've had—what?—forty people in here earlier."

"Well," said Owen, "the place looks the same." He looked around. The peeling support columns still hadn't been painted. The clock reading *Drink Sprite* still ran ten minutes slow. There was nothing on the walls, only the stubble of yellow painted concrete.

"We got about double our membership this month alone," said Jackson. "There's good days ahead, my friend."

There was nothing more to say, which saddened Owen and at the same time thrilled a part of him that had been dormant too long. He was in the arena, and when you were in the arena you focused. A cancerous spleen, a leaking spine, your hemorrhaging eight-year-old at the door: nobody cared. They were here to battle. It was a bracing proposition, and for a moment Owen was nearly moved to tears by the stern and simple beauty of his surroundings.

He rocked on the balls of his feet, studying the position. The shag hair was winning. Surprise. Jackson, though a clumsy tactician, had once battled a California master to a draw. All the boy had to do was slide his queen over. Queen and rook would mate in two moves. Snuff. Owen made a fist and grunted.

The boy picked up his queen and placed it right where Owen had imagined. Jackson, head in his hands, began a slow-motion fidget. "Oh, I've had it now. Can't do this. Can't do that." He waggled his finger at the crucial squares, as if stirring a drink. "Would you *look* at this kid? He's a player."

The shag hair, concentrating, didn't look up. He was long-limbed but slight, and despite his layers of clothing—jean jacket, flannel logger shirt, white T-shirt—his hunched way of sitting made him look mushroomy and soft. Owen took his measure. The boy's pale broad face revealed nothing, a bowl upon which small features had been laid. They looked as if they could shift at any time.

"Okay, I resign," said Jackson pleasantly. He carefully leaned his king over onto its side. "Let's see you two play. You better watch yourself, Owen. This kid's a killer."

The boy looked up. "Are you a master?"

"Near enough."

"He's an expert," said Jackson. "That's right below master."

"I know," the boy said.

Jackson began counting on his fingers. "You got unrated, then you got class rankings. Class E, lowest, then D, C, B, A. Then expert. Master's after that. You're talking better than ninety-nine percent of everyone else."

The boy nodded. Owen without hesitation pushed out his king's pawn. The boy answered in kind, and the game was on.

Jackson continued. "We got, what, like seven or eight masters in the whole state. Owen's *almost* special. And then you got your international categories—"

"Shut up," Owen said, and something sharp in the way he said it quieted Jackson down. The boy played quickly, matching Owen's speed, and not two minutes into the game Owen found himself staggered by a series of slashing, fearless moves. Unbelievable. Owen was rusty, but not that rusty. The boy avoided all his traps and kept the position unbalanced, opening files, baring Owen's king to danger. Now Owen fell into long thinks, balancing his chin on an outstretched thumb, the way the Russian grandmasters sat. On move, he began to crash his weighted chessmen down, loudly, onto their new squares. The intimidation didn't work. The boy shook the hair out of his eyes and crashed his own men down onto new squares. He fell into Owen's rhythm, pausing when Owen paused, responding quickly when Owen made instantaneous replies. It was like playing against a mirror.

And then the boy faltered, sliding his rook over one square too far. A stupid, silly error. Owen could land his knight between the boy's rook and king, winning big material. No sooner did the boy's fingers leave the rook than the boy let out a loud groan.

"Oh my," said Jackson. "I won't say a word."

"You're a player," Owen said forcefully, addressing the boy. "You're doing good." Owen feigned concentration, pretending to look for tricks inside the boy's error. There was no need to be dismissive, smashing the knight onto the killing square. The kid was no fly, no bug to simply swat and forget.

That's how it ended. Owen's hand hovering, the boy toppling his king.

The boy's name was Alex Jacobson. He had never been in a chess club before. His father, he said, had taught him the moves just a few years ago.

Owen stared at the ceiling. "Well, Alex," he said, shifting his gaze to the boy. He leaned forward. "I'll tell you something. You ought to play in some tournaments. I know what I'm talking about. I beat Rassmusson once." Owen paused. "Maybe you got the big gift. I'm thinking maybe you do."

Later, talking on the corner with Jackson and Lonnie, a woman Jackson introduced as his lady, Owen regretted not reviewing his openings before going to the club. After the first game, Jackson had brought out a chess clock from the storeroom, and the three of them played five-minute chess—cutthroat, odd man out—until midnight. They both had crushed Jackson. No one kept count, but even with the kid's ignorance about the Sicilian Defense, especially the Richter-Rauzer line, Owen had been held even, loss for loss, win for win.

It was a moonlit fall night, the clouds tinted gray, thick as turned earth, and an oppressive dampness had settled in. Something small raced across the sidewalk and into the gutter. In the distance, down the hill, squealing tires echoed off the concrete walls. Lonnie was irritated. A friend had dropped her off nearly an hour ago, and she'd been looking at her watch ever since. She was pockmarked and boyishly thin, and she spoke in a deep, whisky-scratch voice that turned to coughing when she laughed.

"Why don't you phone up a cab?" she said sharply.

Jackson had been standing with his hands in his pockets a couple of minutes now. He shrugged. "One'll show up."

"Just phone. There's a phone booth down that way."

"They always show up," said Jackson. "Just a few more minutes."

"Just make sure you tip the driver good," said Owen.

Jackson looked at him. "I'm driving cab these days," said Owen.

"Shit," said Lonnie. She raised her hand as if to strike Jackson. "You play chess all night, then you walk out with a cabbie with no cab. What good are you?"

"No good, I guess," said Jackson.

"He guesses he's no good. Well, that's something anyway."

Jackson blinked. "Not here."

"What's wrong with here?" she said. "I've been standing here half the night, and you didn't seem to mind. I just want a cab." She craned her neck toward some approaching lights. "There's one." She pointed. "Go flag it down."

Jackson lumbered out from the line of parked cars, hands in his pocket, but the taxi sped on down the street.

Lonnie exhaled loudly. "Don't you know how to hail a cab?"

"He didn't see me."

"You didn't stick your arm out. You're supposed to stick your arm out and wave."

"I motioned."

"You did *not*. You just stood there like a lump. Jesus. All I want is a cab. I'm standing here all night and you can't even get me a cab."

"Okay. Calm down."

"I'm calm. That's the trouble. I let you get away with everything. Do you want me to spank your bottom? I think you do."

"Enough. Yes?"

She looked at Owen. "I am so sick of this. I really am. Last week some guy goes, 'Hey sugar, give me some.'" Her mouth turned hard, and she pumped an erect finger at Jackson's stomach. "And this lump just puts his head down."

"What do you want me to do? Get in a fistfight?"

"Yeah, that would be nice. Get in a fistfight. You just stand around and wait. Owen here wouldn't just stand there and wait, would you, Owen?"

"I'm just going home."

She closed her eyes for awhile, and when she opened them again, she was nodding. "Okay. Okay. You don't want to get messed up with a couple of losers. I apologize. I'm calm now. Is there something about chess players? Are you all weirdos? Can you tell me that? You don't look like a weirdo. Tell me you're not a weirdo."

It was suddenly important to Owen to convince her he wasn't a weirdo. There was nothing more important in the world to him right now. Her eyes roamed his face, evaluating, alert. She was looking for a sign, a suggestion, some phrase to assure her she hadn't made another terrible mistake in her life. He told her he'd taken classes at the community college. He read books, worked a job, liked ketchup on his steak, and if that made him weird, then guilty as charged. He spoke in a voice he believed to exude genial wisdom, and he could tell Lonnie was taken with his fresh manner. He said lots of people play chess. Doctors, lawyers, teachers, it crossed all lines. In the Soviet Union, chess was as popular as baseball. There was nothing weird about Russians, was there? People called chess players weird in the U.S., but that was because not many people here played chess. Soon everything was going to change, thanks to Bobby. Soon everyone would be playing chess, and no one would call chess players weird anymore because everyone would be a chess player. Did she see? Did she get it?

Owen paused for effect. Lonnie was listening fiercely. Her eyes focused on some distant point; she pursed her lips as if savoring some word, readying her mouth to repeat it.

Like that kid in the club, he continued. Maybe the kid didn't look like much to people, but really he was something. Maybe another Bobby in a few years. The kid had secret places in him. He was special, always had been probably, and when he became another Bobby everyone would finally know it. Did she see? The kid would *always* have been special, but no one knew.

"That's right." Jackson nodded enthusiastically. "The kid with the hair." He faltered. His hands came out of his pockets and thumped heavily against his pants. Owen could see Jackson wanted to help Lonnie arrive at the correct conclusion but was stuck for how to continue. "Owen here beat him," he said desperately. "He's not making this stuff up."

"Yeah?" she said. She reached into her purse and pulled out a pack of cigarettes. "What's the kid's name?"

"No one's heard of him yet," said Owen. "But he's got what it takes, believe me."

"And you beat him," she said brightly. She lit her cigarette with a tiny silver lighter and pointed the glowing ember toward Owen. "So that makes you pretty smart, doesn't it?"

"Oh, he is," said Jackson.

"I'm a hair's breath from master," Owen said. "I'm not bragging, but you asked."

"Well, here's to you," she said, raising her cigarette as if making a toast. "May you get what you want." There was something erotic in Lonnie's posture and speech, her arm suspended over her head, face upturned, her voice full and throaty, and Owen was suddenly conscious of his quickening blood. Jackson seemed affected too: he looked as though he had just ponied up a turd. He put a big proprietary hand on Lonnie's shoulder. "May you make a pile of money," Lonnie continued. Then she turned to Jackson. "May everyone get to quit their shithole job. May we all get our heart's desire and see everyone's secret places."

"Hear, hear," Jackson said. He smiled.

"Just get me a cab," she said. She slipped her arm around Jackson's back and began stroking. "Okay? We'll walk down the street and you can phone up a cab. All right? That sounds reasonable, doesn't it? We'll just walk down and phone."

They talked awhile longer, just until Lonnie finished her cigarette, and then Owen watched them go and, waving goodbye, he started down the hill toward the district, toward the flaring, drunken shouts, and he was aware in a dim and dreamy way that something had started, a ripple in the water, the single flap of a bird's wing. Back in his room, pipes clanging overhead, Owen had some beers. He stacked the bottle caps on top of each other, shuffling them between his fingers as if they were poker chips. He acknowledged he may have magnified Alex Jacobson's talent. But that was okay. With a groan, he lay down heavily on the bed, ignoring the coughing out in the hall. He had exaggerated in order to go on believing. Not believing in himself, but believing in those secret parts of himself he had not yet discovered. They were still there. They had to be. Not so long ago he thought he would astonish everyone and tear through national tournaments, making a name for himself. He snorted now, cradling his bottle in the crook of one arm, then reached out stiffly with the other arm and formed his fingers into a kind of claw. Air chess. He moved quickly, snapping the invisible chessmen forward, slapping down the plunger of an airy chess clock. He could still make master. Sure. Afterwards . . . who knew?

He sighed. He'd have to start training again. He'd been treating each day as a perpetual present for so long, severing action from consequence, yesterday from today, that training would be hard. He'd have to start tying his days together once more, start gauging his progress, drawing things together into patterns, start comparing, casting himself into a future. Unexpected patterns. New connections. That's what training meant. Finding those things. They were the secret parts of himself that had always been there, the holy places, wild and powerful, enormous, lying in wait like whole continents. But he had to find them. He knew this, had always known it, but the knowledge was so bitter he had chosen to discard what he knew.

He had met his wife at a church mixer, though he himself was not a believer. He was so lonely then there were certain sad songs he feared hearing in public, worried his chin would crinkle, but she was accepting and kind and loved the way his eyes teared up when they kissed in a slow dance. In her tight pink blouse and white nylons, she imprinted herself in his mind. He couldn't stop thinking about her. Winning games, taking home money, he was a proud husband, and he was glad to bring her along to local tournaments, sometimes driving fast up the interstate, or taking a lazy day to wend their way across the border. Her presence was electric. He'd be putting away some old man, some woodpusher, calculating, and she'd come up from behind and start rubbing his shoulders and the whole room would look his way in admiration and desire. He quickly climbed the ranks, class C, class B, class A, low expert, then high expert, right on the verge of master. He was going to quit working his car wash job if he made master. If. He said *if* to friends, but in his heart, whispering to her in bed, he meant *when*. He'd go pro, a man on his way, challenging Benko, Evans, Soltis, all the grandmasters whose photos he touched, day after day, in the pages of *Chess Life*. He'd be surrounded by exotic Germans and Czechs, by rich and powerful patrons, and he'd love her and touch her in ways extravagant and generous and strange.

The knowledge excited in him the sense he was blessed in some indefinable and secret way. He threw himself into studying, into honing his game. He spent enormous sums of money flying or bus-sing to tournaments, to events held first in halls and schools, then in hotels with gleaming balustrades and chandeliers, events always bigger, always more grandiose, than the last. He took the Grey-hound to New York and Philadelphia. He flew to Vegas, Boston, Chicago. But his rating didn't rise. That he wasn't ready to com-pete was pounded into him by some out-of-state master, some man with a burrcut and tattoos. Then in Seattle he lost four out of five games to men of no importance, terrible players. In Phoenix he could only draw class C players. He couldn't go to the next level, and his failure baffled him. He looked to her for a recognition, for some withheld acknowledgment of his secret gift. He waited for her to help him find it, as she had done early on, lending his play a kind of grace, an ease over the board that was spectacular. Waiting, he drank. He stuffed pills in his mouth, smoked weed in the alley by the car wash. He found other women he thought would help him, who could give him back his ease, but they could not help him find his gift either. She left him slowly, bit by bit, first cutting her bountiful red hair as short as a boy's, then withholding her secretary's checks, then going out on the town without him. The more she left, the more betrayed he felt. He blamed her for not supporting him, though he knew it wasn't true; he knew he was to blame, and at the same time he knew he couldn't get up in the morning without her. He was afraid and angry: he fought in bars, went through his money, showed up at the car wash so stoned he cracked someone's windshield with a tire brush. He had words with the regional manager. He lost his job, his car, and then he lost her for good. What a fool he'd been. Waiting, he'd stopped the sequence of moves; he'd stopped being interested in new connections, in unexpected patterns. That's how he lost her. That's how he lost everything. By standing around with his hands in his pockets, eyes fixed and blind, doggedly waiting.

Morning. Owen knew because of the shuffling out in the hall. Sunlight framed the blinds, and he felt hungry for eggs. He'd head on down to the Bay Street Diner, get him some coffee and a three-egg omelet. The hall entryway was clean, the rust and cream chess-board-pattern squares scuffed and wet. The fat man with the orange cap—had it already been a month?—was shaking his push broom into the Dumpster. The man had swept up quite a pile; there was a mound just outside the open door. On top of the dirt lay someone's rippled copy of *Squat Job*, opened to the photo of a woman's grainy spread legs; there were dozens of exploded cigarette butts, two pint bottles of Mad Dog, a hypodermic needle, a crusted yellow bandage and gauze.

Owen, blinking in the light, found himself unable to walk by, to simply leave this terrible garbage in its dusty heap. He stuck out his foot and scooted the magazine and the needle just so, across the rust and cream squares of the entryway, to an approximation of king's four. Then he pushed a cigarette butt over with the sole of his shoe and dragged it over to king's five. The bandages and gauze served as knights; they attacked the king's pawns. He scooted them out to the board. The Mad Dogs became bishops; they attacked the knights. The game was on. King's knight, queen's bishop, pawn up, other pawn up. Owen paused, luxuriating in the small morning breeze, feeling reckless and strong. Big. Like he could live forever.

Out the corner of his eye he saw the janitor approach slowly, the push broom slung over his shoulder like a club. There were some weeds and plant stems on the sidewalk, roots and all. Rhododendrons, sure. Owen couldn't remember where the flowerpots were. The cars out on the interstate sounded like faraway ocean. There was a strong fragrance in the air, something vegetative and sweet. The sun was so bright Owen shielded his eyes. He started walking down the steps. Where is the garden? he asked. The janitor said, Back off motherfuck. The garden, said Owen. Can you tell me? Is the garden still here?

The
Year
Five

Sentimentality, said Nguyen Van Trinh, was the Vietnamese sickness. He had a story to illustrate his point, though over time he
stopped telling it because his own life had made it too ironic. The
story was simple. Back in Vietnam, in the Quang Tri re-education
camp, he was allowed a bamboo sleeping mat to himself twice a
month. Those nights, he laid out the mat just outside the storage
closet, where the cooking pots were piled, to better see the firm,
certain line of the longhouse ridgepole. What was the proverb?
The strong man folds his arms; the wise man shuts his mouth. That
was what the ridgepole said to him; it gave him the strength to live.
So twice a month he stared at the ridgepole until the moonlight
bathed the room in a chalky light and the bird spiders began to
lower, dropping as if by parachute to the floor and scuttling over to
the cooking pots, where they sometimes stroked their abdomens
and detached giant eggsacs that seemed to Trinh's eyes to glow like
distant balls of white-hot phosphorous. His friends, Nguoc and Vu,
both telephone operators from his old unit, did not think of the
nightly visitations in military terms. They were sentimentalists. They
said their hearts were those spiders. What they meant was their

love was delicate as a spider's sac of young. They would bleed for it. They would feed it with their lives.

Twice a month, Trinh woke his friends by flattening the phosphorescent balls with his sandal. He told them he had killed centipedes. He wasn't cruel. He had no wish to mock his friends. He knew sentimentalism was like a disease: it weakened you; it made you susceptible to all manner of spirits and paralysis.

Of course Nguoc and Vu later died—their heads were diseased, they were dreamy as clouds. Trinh lived to flee his ancestral home, his *que huong*, with his only child, his widowed daughter Chi. They left in Year Five—1980, five years since the fall of Saigon—on a crowded wooden boat, the *Binh Huat*, and skirted the Thai coast, sailing all the way down to Malaysia, to the Bidong Island refugee camp, thirty kilometers from the mainland city of Kuala Trengganu. A boy, nephew Duoc, was aboard as well. When the *Binh Huat* arrived, foundering on the camp's Zone C coral, camp security waded out with stretchers. It was never clear when the Thai pirates had boarded. No one pressed the issue. Trinh, Trinh with his nasty wound, had no memory of the attack. He was fortunate to have survived. The boy was too young to give a coherent account. Chi was found laid out in the hold, with the others.

Her death was what made his story too ironic for telling. It gave him the Vietnamese sickness, and now the sickness was killing him.

On Bidong, it was difficult not to think like a sentimentalist. Every day the loudspeakers played Vietnamese folk songs and announced arrivals and departures. No one knew how many boat people— boat people! even the American term was sentimental—no one knew exactly how many people were there, waiting on the tiny island for the Americans or the French or the Australians to shuttle them out. The relief workers said thirty thousand, but they always rounded up, to get more funding.

Thirty thousand. Decency, Trinh said, demanded a specific number. So he kept a private tally of all the young women. With every
new face, his heart raced; his hands would move, fingers trembling,
poised as if for seduction. He had to stop after a week. He had
begun to imagine Chi in their strangers' clothes, Chi carrying a
basket of cuttlefish, perhaps bored, slapping a fly away from her
nose. If decency demanded a specific number, then what if, say,
number 317 could trade places with her—some girl with a blank
face, a beetle-nut chewer, a skinny moonflower with hands like
bark? What if he could have Chi back? He imagined ocean, a clean,
blue horizon, one without mess: the beetle-nut chewer would drop
swiftly, her face full of surprise, lungs flapping like balloons, a word
exploding at last from her tight lips. *Water*, she would say. Once,
touching a girl on the arm, he said the word out loud. He knew
he'd said it only when he saw her expression. Then he had to turn
away, to hide his face. His sickness shamed him. It had turned him
ghoulish.

He had heard that sentimentality let Vietnamese endure their
history. Perhaps that was true. The air in camp was putrid, heady
with the gases from the sewage canals that ran through camp, and
in the evening, the rats emerged from their burrows and began to
squeal and shimmy up the sapling posts in the refugee huts. Then
the Malay Task Force guards walked their rounds, spitting and hacking, and their flashlights shined right and left, like headlights on
runaway cars. They were looking for women. The old people would
look away, rubbing eucalyptus oil on their arms. What else could
they do? How else could they endure? The old people would nod,
saying the night smelled like the Chinese carnivals back in Vietnam, in the Delta, back when the French marched smartly through
the streets with tassels dangling from their hats.

In those days, at the mid-autumn festivals, people said, before
the water spirit and the land spirit began their seasonal battle out in
the paddy, you could see magicians glowing in the orange light of
paper lanterns. The magicians wore pointed Siamese hats and

turned bean-curd dumplings into dragonfly wings and blood-red petals, then led the crowds to a porcelain table where a tiny man peering through a microscope cut a rice grain into a hundred pieces. The tiny man waved his customers over and had them press their eyes to the microscope lens to see the miraculous tiny specks of rice swimming on the specimen slide. "They're alive," the tiny man said. "Cut a grain of rice into pieces, and you'll see. They're looking for each other." People smiled and chuckled. The schoolteachers among them knew the tiny man had swirled the solution with a toothpick and the specimens were riding in currents, but it was wonderful to imagine the chopped-up rice as families broken apart, swimming the ocean in search of loved ones. It was wonderful to imagine, so that was what the schoolteachers did, and everyone slept that night quiet and peaceful as toads.

So beautiful, to be a sentimentalist. The old people, they floated on a silver string between the past and the present. They drifted in the air, light as kites, and at night they watched the fires die down and barely stirred when rats squealed in the huts and ran out the sugar-bag doors with mouthfuls of cabbage or skin.

They were dangerous, these sentimentalists.

Nguyen Van Trinh, diseased, knew himself to be dangerous. His mind was lying.

His first sight of the camp, or so the social workers told him, had been the dense wall of garbage, high as a man's waist, spread in mashed layers the length of the Zone C beach, all the way from the shale abutment bordering Zone D to the UN compound at the other end. At the time, he was said to be drifting in and out of consciousness, severely sunburned, a crusted slit running from the top of his head to his chin. He was lifted roughly from the boat by his swollen ankles and bright red arms by two Vietnamese men with special white badges who stared at his blistered body and said to no one in particular that he shouldn't have left in such a small boat in October.

What he remembered was a solid crust of yellow-green pineapple husks, swirling brown cabbage, and twisted red Marlboro cartons, under which he glimpsed strips of cloth and blue tarp winding in and out like ribbons, and glistening, creamy pockets of white and yellow; and just under the surface, he saw the silvery glints of aluminum, diaphanous claw membranes, tiny alabaster bones and cartilage, speckled grayfish skin, and lengths of pink yarn, all supported by foundations of crumbly gray and brown whose makeup over time had grown impossible to determine. He was carried through a path in a wall of garbage, but because he had been infected, because he had the Vietnamese sickness, his mind did not understand what his eyes saw. He nearly cried out, for so constant in texture were the layers, so unexpected in delicacy and color, the gummy bubble of air hanging over the beach seemed suddenly not rancid but sweet, and the bloated cloud of bluebottles descending on garbage and human alike seemed the languorous, tickly black down of fluffy store-bought pillows.

There, to either side, was layer after layer, grown to enormous size, of his daughter's gaily colored wedding cake made years ago by a famous Saigon chef, the cake Chi's new husband had wheeled in himself on a trolley cart to demonstrate for his bride the extravagance of his love. In her lace dress and misty veil and gold, tear-shaped jewelry, Chi had looked so beautiful and new that even when she offered her father a slice of cake on a paper plate he did not trust himself to speak for fear of bursting into tears of joy. He nodded his head and sat stiffly in his chair, and when she knelt at his feet and placed her hand on his to guide his fingers over the red plastic fork, she whispered into his ear that she was grateful for his happiness because he was her father and had always treated her well and had never before eaten cake. She placed the morsel on his tongue, and his hand trembled with excitement in hers, for he had not expected to hear her declaration, or to feel the huge square dissolve so quickly in his mouth, or to hear his new son-in-law clap American soldiers on the back and cheer at his chewing, or to see his sister wipe at his shirt with the lace-fringed handkerchief she kept in a box with her jewelry. And when each mouthful of the rich cake slid down his throat, he moaned with pleasure and weepy astonishment that he should be sitting in a white metal chair with his plate on a tablecloth in a room at the best restaurant in the district, where Americans in shiny blue uniforms applauded and his sister from Phan Tiet clucked her tongue and fussed with his shirt and columns of light laced through the window and onto the small golden hand of his beautiful Chi, who fed him cake with a red plastic fork.

So it was that on the Zone C beach Trinh thrust his head toward the wall of garbage and opened his mouth. He felt his body slip from the grasp of the men wearing special white badges, and when his head touched the sand he clawed at the ground and lunged into the wall, sinking his teeth into the layers of green and pink before him. He chewed, he felt it on his tongue, and then he swallowed, tasting in the layers something so sweet that even one of the men wearing a special white badge could not pry open his mouth to scrape out what he was eating.

When later he lay in a bunk in a long line of bunks that he recognized to be an arrangement found in a hospital, he tapped the gauze strips wrapped like a helmet around his head. He clucked his tongue. He listened. He heard the shuffling of sandals along the wood floor, the tinny scrape of metal pans, the soft Delta accents. Off to the right, ever so clearly, he heard a voice exclaim loudly over the size of a white nurse who had apparently lumbered past. It was Duoc. His nephew Duoc. The boy was ten and already coarse as a dog.

"Chi," Trinh said, pressing his fingers into the gauze. "Chi." He listened. He heard a ceiling fan. "Chi," he said. He heard a chainsaw far away, and he heard someone complain about a swollen arm. He heard a plastic bag full of liquid drop to the floor. He heard the ocean nearby. And then his head was full of birds, and the birds were squawking and pulling at his eyes and his ears, and he tossed on his side and quite by accident pulled out a plastic tube that had been inserted into his arm. He thrashed around, balling his hands into fists. He pounded his bedsheet. A Vietnamese woman wearing a white T-shirt and loose black pants ran to his bunk and told him to lie still. She looked at him sternly, fiddling with a drip bottle connected to the tube that had fallen from his arm.

"*Ngu di*," she said. "Sleep."

Trinh stared. The set of her mouth, the wispy hairs that moved around her throat, the graceful curve of her nose—all looked like Chi's. He held his arms out stiffly, as if to receive a package, and with a moan so loud it caused the nurse to step away, rolled onto his back and shut his eyes and rocked his head back and forth. The nurse leaned over and whispered into his ear that she was sorry to hear about his daughter, but when loved ones died it made sense to rest.

So he did. When he awoke, he smelled the garbage on his breath.

For days he was content to stare at the ceiling fan whirring overhead and eat rice gruel served in a blue plastic bowl by a pretty girl from Binh Tuy Province. As the fan blades moved, he thought of Chi's hair flapping in the wind aboard the boat. He pictured the boat on the Gulf of Siam. How long did they float? Two weeks? Three? He wasn't sure. He saw himself sitting on a bench in the storage hold. Chi was beside him. Nephew Duoc sat on the opposite bench. The boy smelled. Trinh had taken him along—a burden, a hateful, screaming child—only as a favor to his sister. He remembered shouting at Duoc not to drink all their water. He remembered the boy stealing a cup from Chi's hand and pouring it down his throat. Why had he ever agreed to take him? He had slapped the boy, cursed him; and then he comforted Chi, stroking her hair, and told her the captain would bring them more water soon. He remembered showing the captain, a silk merchant, how to read the French compass. He remembered standing in a line of men, pulling a rope coiled around the generator. He had cheered when the motor stuttered with the sound of firecrackers. He remembered the ocean lunging at the hull. The water seeped through the planks and tickled their toes; at night, it licked their ears and bathed their eyes. He remembered the boat tilting. In the morning, Thais in a high-keeled boat came to save them. The Thais secured a line to their railing. They gave his shipmates a clamp for the bilge line. They clasped their hands together and touched their heads in greeting.

Then there was nothing. Just buzzing, like dragonflies hovering. Buzzing, and then her beautiful cake.

He lay in his hospital bunk perfectly straight for hours on end, imagining himself embalmed, laid out as if on display in a mausoleum. He would not say a word. His tongue felt out of place, like an extra limb. The Vietnamese woman in the T-shirt and loose black pants—a slip of paper pinned to her shirt identified her as a nurse— came by every day in the morning and afternoon to change his dressing and tape down the plastic tube that ran from a jar into his arm. "How are you?" she'd say in Vietnamese. "Have you eaten rice yet? Did you land in Zone C? Do you want me to bring your nephew over?" When she asked the questions, she bent down, hovering inches from his face. She smiled, radiating cheer. In answer, he slowly turned his head to the right, wincing as the stems of the chicken feathers in his small pillow pinched his ears. His neighbor was a young boy who always had his legs under a tented bedsheet. The boy would try to catch his eye, but Trinh always looked at the boy's stained mattress. Then the nurse would walk around Trinh's bunk, idly tapping his feet with the pen she carried in her pants' pocket, and ask the same questions on the other side. Trinh would turn his head to the left. His neighbor to that side was a tight-faced Chinese man. The man always had his arm resting on his forehead, so Trinh figured the man had a fever; they never looked at each other. The nurse would sigh, then walk around to other side of Trinh's bunk, tapping his feet with her pen. She would frown, wiggling her pen, then bend over to hover inches from his face and repeat her questions.

Each day the rows of patients across from Trinh sat up in their beds to watch the performance. The nurse would ask questions; Trinh would turn his head. Back and forth they went, asking and turning, always the same. In the mornings, with the sunlight slanting in from the slat windows and relatives ambling through the ward, clucking their tongues and pointing, the patients pulled for the nurse. *Grab his head*, they'd say. *Twist his finger. Tell him to talk to his nephew.* In the evening the slat windows were shut and the fluorescent lights crackled off and on. The relatives were not allowed in; the stench from the honey pots under their beds filled the ward. The patients, bored, changed their allegiance. As the nurse walked around his bed, back and forth, they shouted out encouragement to Trinh. *Here comes the cat*, they'd say. *Left side. Plug your ears. Put a bandage over your mouth.*

Then a white woman with UNHCR sewn into her T-shirt began to bring his nephew Duoc over in the mornings. She had blond hair stacked up in a bun. The boy's hand was encircled by hers; with his free hand he stroked the downy blond hairs on her arm. Trinh could not bear to look at him. The boy was not the flesh of his flesh. Yet he had survived the journey well. The sunburn gave his skin a healthy glow. The nurse had given him a spinning top painted to look like a girl in a conical hat. The sight was infuriating.

Every morning the white woman brought the boy. Every morning Trinh turned his head away. His neighbors lost patience. "He's your nephew," the patients shouted. They sat up in their bunks, craning their necks like chickens. "Say hello to your nephew, old man," they said. "Are you a brick?" Trinh rubbed the gauze dressing around his head and stared straight into the fan blades rotating above. "A pig's heart," the patients said. They pointed him out to their relatives. He could feel their eyes on him, but still he would not speak to Duoc. One morning Duoc stood with the white woman at the foot of his bed. Trinh heard him say he was going to live in the Zone F longhouses until his uncle felt better. The patients clucked loudly as the boy walked away, rubbing the white woman's arms. "Pickle-hearted old man," the patients said. Trinh heard them. He drew up his pillow around his head, and the words went away.

The next morning he ate his rice gruel spooned in by the pretty girl from Binh Tuy and looked up at the whirling fan on the ceiling, and he felt his face fold like an accordion. The girl drew back. She put the spoon in the bowl and excused herself. "My breakfast," he called out. "I'm not finished." Everyone looked up. Trinh could not control his voice. It was louder than he had intended; it cracked. The white woman with UNHCR sewn into her T-shirt came running down the hall, followed by a Vietnamese orderly. "Okay," the white woman said. "Okay. Take it easy. You're absolutely fine. It's perfectly natural. Let it come, Mr. Trinh. Let it come all you want." She bent over his bunk and told him to breathe naturally, but he was diseased and couldn't stop crying.

When the gauze strips came off, he received a camp ID from the Malay Task Force guards and stood in line every day with everyone else to receive packets of rations. The rice was full of stones and weevils; the salt was wet; the cans of peas no one would touch for fear of getting diarrhea. He shared his rations with Duoc, who, over his objections, had been assigned to live with him in Zone A. Together they slept in a lean-to of corrugated tin and blue plastic tarp, and they wore black running shorts selected by the Zone A Vietnamese administration chief. Occasionally Duoc brought in onions. He quietly placed the offerings by the fire pit where they sat in the morning to boil water. Trinh did not know where Duoc got the supplies. He supposed the boy stole them. He did not ask. He knew only that the onions filled the shelter with a smell far more pleasant than the latrines in neighboring Zone B.

Every morning Trinh scooped the rat droppings from the dirt floor with a palm frond. He made rice in the fire pit and gave Duoc half, then took the blue plastic bowls to the Zone A beach, where he dunked them in the ocean and scraped them clean. He wrote long letters to the resettlement delegations on wispy blue paper, detailing his hatred for communists. He wrote poems in the margins of newspapers, tearing them out and staring, then folding the strips into his pocket. He listened for the hourly chimes that rang from the loudspeakers hung in the trees. At the tenth chime he walked down the footpath to the social services division office, where white women wearing UNHCR T-shirts talked to him for half an hour. Each day they wrote question marks on tiny yellow stickers and pressed them onto the pages of his record file. The next day another white woman would read the yellow stickers and take them off.

The sessions were almost always the same. One day a large blond woman wearing glasses shook his hand. She asked him to sit down. "Tell me about your family," the woman said.

"Who is your family?" asked her translator, a thin Vietnamese boy who lived in Zone F.

"I speak better English than he does," said Trinh, pointing to the boy.

"If he's not translating right," said the woman, "just tell me and I can ask the question again." She took off her glasses and put them in her blouse pocket. "It's his job, Mr. Trinh. Please. Let's just talk."

"I already told the other woman," Trinh said.

"Tell me," she said.

Trinh told her he had had a daughter, Chi. She died on the boat, at sea.

"He used to have a daughter," said the translator. The social worker smiled. "The lady is happy," said the translator, turning to Trinh. The social worker held up a paper-clipped note.

"Somebody wrote," she said, "that you can't recall the events. Is that right?"

"Who wrote to you?" said the translator.

Trinh looked at the translator hard.

"Help us help you," said the social worker.

"The lady wants your help," said the translator.

The social worker leaned forward, conspiratorially. "If there's a wound," she said, tapping her head, "an *invisible* wound, up here, we can help you rinse it clean."

"If you're shot," said the translator, "they'll wash you."

Trinh laughed. "You're right," he told the woman. "I can't remember."

"It's important that you do," said the woman. She pulled the glasses from her pocket and held them by the earpieces. "Do you believe that?"

"She is not a liar," said the translator. Trinh slapped the boy on the arm.

The woman frowned. She told Trinh to rise. He did. Then he walked with her and the translator to the Zone C beach. The woman's arm was draped over Trinh's shoulders. She pointed at the ocean, then at the beach. "This is where you arrived," she said. "Right here in Zone C, in front of the rubbish."

Trinh looked out over the beach, where garbage still lay mashed in dense, even layers as high as his knees. He cupped his nose with his hands.

"Do you remember?" the social worker asked. "Try with all your heart."

The translator swept his arm toward the horizon. "Tell her your memory," he said.

Trinh only shrugged. The three stood on the beach a moment, looking at the engine hulks and boat frames piled up near the coral. "Poor Mr. Trinh," said the woman. She had Trinh and the translator follow her back. In the office, she pressed small yellow stickers onto the pages of his record file. "Poor Mr. Trinh," she said, squeezing his hand.

Trinh spoke. Might a man, he said, might a man walk on the Zone C beach and lay his foot into a shovel and by a powerful thrust of his mind remove himself from the heat and the noise and the bluebottles and the terrible smell and slice through the layers and put the shovel to his lips and taste a wonderful sweetness, such as found in wedding cake? Then he was quiet. He saw the look in her eyes. He held her hand, he swung it gaily, like a lover might, and he told her he had been sick; the talk of the ill was just straw on the roof to keep out the rain. Really, he said. Really. Believe me. Just straw on the roof. There was no need to tell anyone.

Late at night when the children began to howl and the tide rushed in with the sound of pebbles, Trinh heard the rats scrabble in and out of the tunnels and nests they had clawed into the Zone C garbage. He heard them squeal like bats when the Malay Task Force guards raked their flashlight beams across the beach from behind rusty bales of concertina wire separating their barracks from the Western staff and the shelters of the Vietnamese. Night after night he awoke with a jolt when he sensed their small pink eyes scanning the shelter and heard them plop from the rafters and race toward his cardboard bed.

One night he walked to the far end of the Zone C beach to feel the wind and hear the great sheets of ocean rush in. He stood atop an engine hulk to better see the long dark border that outlined the garbage on the beach, marking where the tide licked at its edges. He clutched his shirt in astonishment when he saw the border was not the seaweed he had always assumed, but a rim of spiky gray fur and stiffened tails from rats recently pressed by sheer numbers off the cusp of the garbage. For weeks he told people over and over what he had seen.

"Rats," he said. "Imagine so many rats. Eating that filth."

"This is all you say," said his neighbor. "All the time. Can't you shut up?" The neighbor made crabpots from cylinder heads and saplings. Each morning, he left little wet piles of crab shell outside his hut.

"Eating filth," said Trinh, scowling. "Disgusting."

The man looked at him in irritation. "*You* ate it," he said. "I was there. I saw you. You ate filth."

Trinh stared. He heard the man's words; he knew the words were true. He stood with his hands at his sides. He couldn't raise them. He opened his mouth to speak, but nothing came out.

The tiny boats continued to pile onto the beaches, and the men in special white badges lifted the bodies onto the beach and grabbed the arms of those who could walk until the lilting sounds of Vietnamese rose over the ocean. The refugees made shelters of branches and tarp, and stood in lines for rations of rice and cabbage and processed chicken. There were so many arrivals, the island was rumored to be sinking under their weight. The refugees stripped Zone B of its underbrush, leaving a naked orange gouge stretching from the beachfront to the top of the five-hundred-meter hill in the center of the island. The garbage on the Zone C beach had grown so immense the rat specialist brought in from Hong Kong announced with much head-shaking from the bow of the UN speedboat that the rat population was threatened only by heart disease. The rats were becoming obese, he said. More relief workers came, and the Malaysian Task Force contingent doubled overnight. The loudspeakers blared music and English lessons and announcements from morning to night.

Trinh wanted only to work. When he worked, his body ached and his skin felt tough as hide but his mind was clear as sky. He heard Mr. Hong's construction division was short of men. He helped build a dock from the planks that had been stripped off the hundreds of boats littering the beaches, jutting from the sand like giant black cheroots. He carried wood. He hammered nails in the walls of the new schools and the administration building. He hefted plastic pipes on his back. He dug trenches and pulled on a chain to lower a black water-storage tank into a hole. He put up plank frames for latrines, though many of his neighbors still preferred to use the slit trench behind the cemetery. At night, he unfolded strips of newsprint and stared at the poems he had scribbled in the margins, and in the glow of the fire-pit embers he wrote more and folded them into his pocket and licked the ink off his fingers so no one would know he had been writing.

He worked hard, and because he worked so hard he was chosen to work in the hospital, which had recently been outfitted with kerosene lamps and donated hospital beds from the *Ile de Lumière*, a French hospital ship anchored offshore. On Sundays he rose early with the white hospital staff to empty diseased organs and amputated limbs into plastic bags he then dumped into the ocean from the back of the water barge that brought supplies once a week. In his free time, he walked around the community center in Zone C, where he helped dispense supplies. Sometimes, when no one was looking, he slipped string into his pocket, as a present for Duoc. He played with the boy, holding the string high in the air. Duoc leaped like a cat. Snot dripped from his nose.

"Jump," Trinh said. "Jump." The boy did.

"Now beg," said Trinh. The boy squatted and mewled. They laughed.

So this is forgiving, Trinh thought. It was so easy. It was like sleeping.

Trinh was elected assistant chief of the community center, a post that gave him permission to visit the Western staff in their new compound and use one of their toilets if he were in the compound at the time he needed it. He moved with Duoc to Zone C, where a man leaving that day for France sold him a shelter for the price of a carton of Malaysian 555 cigarettes. In his new shelter, the bed was a platform of smooth wood. The walls were bright blue tarp

donated by the UN. The door was made of hewn branches lashed
together with hemp. And the roof. The new roof was his joy. It was
a long zinc sheet, secured with spikes. There were no fronds to fall
to the dirt floor. There would be no rain soaking his clothes.

At the beginning of the monsoon season, trouble started in the
community center. Equipment began to disappear. And so he
watched with great interest one evening as a Swedish social worker
pointed her long finger at his friend Miss Lai, whom she accused
of hiding sewing bobbins from the Chinese women in Zone F.
Miss Lai denied the charge and feared she would be reported to
the Malaysian police, who would cancel her interview with the
American refugee delegation. Her mother and father were in Texas,
and in her fear she could only say the word *Texas* over and over.
When the Swede shook her head and held up a sewing bobbin,
Miss Lai began to rock and moan and shiver violently, much to the
confusion of the Swedish social worker, who began to cry in sympathy. Miss Lai went down on all fours. Her shiny polyester shirt
glistened like a shell. Trinh felt a sudden whooshing in his head.
He had to turn away. He closed his eyes to stop from seeing; he
pounded his ears to stop from hearing; he bit his tongue to stop
from speaking. He ran outside and saw in the brilliant sunset the
same beautiful magenta and blue and ribboned gold and whites
and greens he had seen on his daughter's wedding cake many years
ago.

He folded his arms and walked to his shelter. When he pulled
the tarp aside, Duoc shouted into his ear to surprise him. He grabbed
the boy's arm and slapped his face. The boy ran out in fear,
and inside, masked by the tarp walls, Trinh put his hands to his
head and fell to his knees and began to eat dirt. He ate and he ate,
he felt the paste slide down his throat, and when later that night
warm rain drenched the camp, he did not notice Duoc sleeping in
the corner, he did not hear the young men outside complaining
and trudging through the mud with palm fronds over their heads,
in search of wood and leaves to patch their leaky shelter roofs. To

him, the rain thumping the zinc overhead was the pounding of a powerful diesel motor. In the blackness of early morning, the rain came down so hard, the pylons on the dock shook loose. His roof seemed to roar. He fell from his bunk onto the damp floor, and he heard the *clack-clack-clack* of engine tappets. The dirt underfoot: was it dirt? It was hard and grainy. It stung like sea salt. It was a deck, and he was squatting on it. He smelled ocean. And there were the Thais, lounging on board. They had brought a bucket over from their own boat. The bucket was filled with ice cubes the Thais gave to the children, and when the bucket was depleted they had another bucket brought aboard. The Thais would not leave. Their line remained secured, and the railing tires lashed to the two boats came together with each wave, making a sound like kissing. Trinh saw the Thais talk together in a tight circle. He turned to talk to Chi; he grabbed an ice cube from the bucket; he put his hands in his pocket. And when he turned around he saw the Thais had the faces of demons. They spoke in demon language. They breathed demon breath into his face. They pounded the deck with their feet and waved their cleavers and parangs over their heads. They hacked off the top of a melon and threw pulp on the deck. They threw a cooking pot over the railing. Tiny blue veins bulged from their necks. They opened the wheelhouse door and pushed the captain down the steps leading into the hold, and then the demons swarmed the deck. Trinh closed his eyes to stop from seeing; he pounded his ears to stop from hearing; he bit his tongue to stop from speaking. He could do nothing. He stood there, and they came. He could do nothing at all. And when three hours later the demons had exhausted their strength, he pressed his hand against the slit on his scalp and stood in the pilothouse, staring, where the demons had hacked his daughter's throat to the bole and left her sprawled on a bench, dressed only in a black shirt that grew shiny from her blood.

When the rain let up, he woke Duoc.

He shook his nephew so hard, the boy shouted. Trinh threw aside the sugar-bag door, holding Duoc's hand tight. Even in the rain, the cigarettes of the young men lit up the camp like thousands of fireflies, and Duoc, seeing his uncle's face briefly in the faint light, squirmed in his grasp, crying softly. Trinh had on his very best white shirt, which he had ironed and creased himself, just last week, by placing heated rocks in a can. He wore flip-flops and his only pair of socks, which he almost never wore. Socks were impractical and hot, but he kept the pair anyway because they had come in a package from the UN, and they were soft as a girl's hand pressed to his cheek. The two stepped onto the smooth basalt in front of their shelter and walked past a woman skinning a rat that had been skewered on a branch. They took the muddy trail leading down the hill, into the main camp. They came to a wider footpath and hurried past the shelters, a jumble of blue and gray, some two stories high, as rickety and ingenious as monstrous houses of cards, then took the bald scalloped trail that led up the side of Religion Hill. The loudspeakers blared Paul Anka, then "The Tennessee Waltz," and the smell of cloves and oil soaked into their pores. They walked past the market, past the barbed-wire bales nipping at the backs of the cigarette sellers and the toothless old women who fingered joss sticks and running shorts piled high on desks donated by Malaysian schoolchildren in Kuala Trengganu.

In Trinh's pocket were the poems he had written, and a shiny black comb that was his only remaining possession from his boat journey from Vietnam. This he now removed from his pocket and raked firmly along the cheek of young Duoc, leaving a flaring red line that caused the boy to put his fingers to his face and stop making noise. Now silent, they continued past a Swede and an American sitting on the bright yellow porch of a bungalow in the staff compound, intent on a board game, then past a group of barechested boys floating boats carved from Clorox bottles in the sewer, which, before the monsoons, had moved over a thousand pounds of shit from Zone A to Zone D each day before clogging up at the narrow lichen-filled passage in Zone E and forcing the Vietnamese sanitation-division men to use long hookpoles to move the sewage along.

Far from the sewer, up the side of Religion Hill, were stands of coconut trees growing so close together the palms seemed to blot the sun from the sky, turning the ground so dark children would drop to their knees to pretend they were anteaters trapped in a cave or rabbits hiding from the clouds that towered like mountains over the ocean and drenched the whole island in rain. Nguyen Van Trinh and his nephew Duoc walked into the coconut stands, past the giant white carving of a sail, past the Buddha carved by a famous Saigon artist, past the English classroom where the blackboard had been stolen by men believed to have later drowned in a homemade fishing boat.

Trinh, diseased, enraged by the Vietnamese sickness, selected a tree. He swore at Duoc and shook his fist in the boy's face, and with threats and curses forced his nephew up into the tree, which the boy climbed with the ease of a monkey. He yelled at the boy to climb to the top, to the point where the palm fronds blocked out the sky, and he told him to shake the branches. Trinh planted his feet and squinted. He watched the swaying husks. *Again*, he shouted. A coconut thudded at his feet. *Again. Again.* He positioned himself, and he stood very still, and when the coconut that would hemorrhage his skull broke free it did not seem as much to fall as to hurtle, and then Trinh went down hard. When at last the men in special white badges responded to the siren wails of the boy, they found the poems in Trinh's pocket and showed them to the white people and the Malays. Power is greater than love, the Vietnamese said, translating slowly. Each poem was the same. Power is greater than love, power is greater than love, power is greater than love.

Gurmit Singh, the camp's new Malaysian Red Crescent Society administration chief, was already imagining the skin around his eyes grown bunched as a washcloth. The two women wanted the form filled out, and he felt helpless to refuse them. What with the smell, the bluebottles hovering outside, the loudspeaker racket: he couldn't get his bearings. Even the trip from the mainland had been unsettling. The Malay supply boat captain had sat hunched on a stool, guiding the craft with his bare feet, toes looped like fingers around spokes in the pilotwheel. He told Gurmit there were so many water jugs and pots caught in the coral these days that his neighbors just waded out and supplied their kitchens. The debris, said the captain, was Vietnamese. He was testing. His expression asked, *Are you tender?* With the camp in view, the captain started in again. Boats out of Vinh Binh, he said, had been skirting the east coast of Malaysia all year, and when the waves roared, the boat people threw their belongings overboard to lighten the load. Sometimes they panicked so much they even threw cigarettes away. And then he tossed Gurmit a pack of Pall Malls. "Light up," he said in Malay. On Bidong the cigarettes tasted of sea salt.

Now, seated in the supply building, Gurmit frowned. The form on his desk was red.

"How can?" he said. He leaned forward, as if by dint of concentration to make the form go away. He wore a dazzling white safari suit, purchased in Kuala Trengganu with advance pay from his new position. His pockets were full of jackfruit and plastic baggies—who knew the food situation on Bidong?—and around his neck was an ornamental Sikh dagger, given to him by his father.

"Can," said the Malay clerk. Her name was Norizalina. Beside her sat Bobbi Sortini, a teacher-slash-jack of all trades with the UN. At least so she had introduced herself on the Zone C dock.

"Lucky boy," said Bobbi. She played with the straps of her overalls. "Your first executive decision. Admin's never been my cup of tea. You know?"

"I cannot," said Gurmit, rapping his finger on the form.

"Can-*lah*," said Norizalina.

"You can," said Bobbi. "Unless you want the hospital staff calling for your head. They say . . . what's his name again?"

"Nguyen Van Trinh," said Norizalina.

"They say his body's been stinking up the hospital for days. The Vietnamese nurses had to throw lime on him."

"Terrible," said Gurmit.

"Right. So we've got to put him under. For health reasons if nothing else. Now I've already told you the only way to get coffin wood is to fill this out." She laid her hand on the form. "Fill it out and have the supply boat take it back to the mainland. Nobody in Kuala Trengganu moves without it."

"There is another way?" Gurmit asked.

"*Tidak*," said Norizalina firmly. "No."

"It's just a form," said Bobbi. "History of Deceased. That's all. Nothing unsavory."

"I am thinking unsavory," said Gurmit.

"Then where are you going to get the wood, Gurmit?" said Bobbi. "The boats have already been stripped. We can't fell any trees. Not since your government decreed us liable for property."

"Is a prison camp," said Norizalina. "Illegal aliens, yes?"

"Yes," said Gurmit. "I am aware."

"And Supply tells me they're out of plywood," said Bobbi. "So."

"But we are knowing nothing of Nguyen Van Trinh?" said Gurmit.

"Not a damn thing," said Bobbi. She stirred. "I'm sorry. That didn't come out right. But you've got to realize a lot of the suicides here are like that. They've been traumatized at sea. Sometimes they . . . I don't know, *disappear* when they arrive. Like there's no one there, you know?"

"No ID with the body-*lah*," said Norizalina. "No one claims relation. His nephew too young. Task Force cannot find records."

"So," said Bobbi.

"Can do," said Norizalina, tapping the form.

"I'll tell you what," said Bobbi. "We'll leave you to your decision. But I just don't see what else you can do. It's got to be done. You know, *I'd* be doing it if you hadn't arrived. It's about time we got an admin chief."

"I would do, too," said Norizalina. "No other way."

The women turned and made for the door, shuffling in their sandals.

"Now you've got what you need in that pile right there, yes?" said Bobbi, opening the door. She pointed to the stack of red folders on the corner of the desk.

They didn't wave going down the steps. Nor did he. The air was suddenly stifling. Gurmit fiddled with the top button of his safari suit, breathing deeply. He shrugged. He could hear sing-songy Vietnamese spoken outside, and somewhere in the distance a chainsaw started up. There didn't seem to be any noise coming from the dock, except for the revving of the boat engine. He heard crackling nearby, and then the sound of guitars and singing. It was "Proud Mary," blaring from a point just behind him, overhead. He looked up. Through a hole cut in the ceiling, in the corner, two cables dangled down to the floor and into a patchwork of duct tape by the door.

He placed one hand on the History of Deceased form and the other on the pile of red folders, and felt the noise vibrate through his shirt. The wall planks were buzzing to the beat, stirring dust, and heat seemed to rise in waves from the floorboards.

He had to have air. He leaned back and fiddled with the louver handle on the window frame, then stuck his nose through the open slats. Young women in flowered pajamas were milling around the Zone C garbage dump, putting cloth to their noses. From the other side, out along what he assumed to be Zone D, Vietnamese boys ran in the sand, straining like swimmers, and a Malay Task Force guard on the dock steps waved his truncheon like a broom, shooing people away. A great cloud of diesel smoke issued from the back of the supply boat, bringing the boat captain out of the pilothouse. He began pounding a screwdriver against a metal box outside the door. A bullhorn lay on the deck, atop wicker baskets of brown cabbage. Bluebottles shimmered over the cargo.

Gurmit pictured himself back in Kuala Trengganu, sitting in a crumbling Chinese theater, tilting his head at the screen, sweating, just chewing durian gum and watching. Like a bloody schoolboy, he thought. Always the bloody schoolboy. Just watching things pass by, frame by frame. He felt something like panic, though it wasn't panic; it was something raging and feverish, something that made him want to dump the form on the floor and wag his finger at Bobbi and Norizalina and run on the beach and slap the Viets and the guards and tell everyone to start over.

"Bloody hell," he said. He sat quietly a moment, hands spread over the History of Deceased form. Then he reached into the pile of red folders to his right and extracted one at random from the middle. The folder was a man's. A burn victim, dead since last April. Gurmit scanned the sheets quickly. The information would do. He laid the folder out on the desk. He began. Word for word, he copied the information onto Nguyen Van Trinh's form. Date of birth, family affiliation, employment, province: all lies. But the women were right. Nguyen Van Trinh had to be put in a box. The Kuala Trengganu office could ship the coffin wood out in half a day. Not that an hour here or there made much difference. In a few minutes Nguyen Van Trinh would never even have existed.

He completed the form. He sat. He looked out the window, composing his face.

Gurmit Singh, son of Gopal Singh, was the only Sikh on Bidong. It was his fate to be alone, he concluded, because it had always been so. His lineage traced back to a noble line of Sikh warriors. Two generations back, Sikhs by the thousands had left the spare land of northern India for the promise of honorable money to be made tin mining in what was then British-ruled Malaya. His grandfather had arrived at the head of the Klang River, in the state of Selangor, and given his passport to a white man who promised sixty ringgit in pay every month. The money never appeared. Gurmit's grandfather fell silent with shame. With glowering eyes he spent his days under the thumb of a Chinese straw boss, who put him to work moving mounds of dirt from the bottom of the Tan Huat strip mine to the top in order to pay for his working papers. One day at the rim of the mine he looked up and saw a white man in a pith helmet and white shorts. He was sure it was the man who had taken his passport. He seized his chance and swung his shovel over his head, crying out that only dogs pawed at the earth and that he was not a dog, for only a man could speak such words. He was clubbed from behind for his impertinence and woke to find himself alone in the back of a lorry loaded with giant bloody sacks of chicken feet. He praised Allah and Vishnu and Jesus for his deliverance and hired on in the driver's family business, where until his death at the age of seventy, he cleaved away the feet of chickens piled high as laundry and threw the stems into a giant bloody sack tied to his waist.

Gurmit's father, a melon hawker, had found deliverance as well. Every day he set up his melon cart twenty-seven paces from the doorway of the Malayan Banking Corporation in Kuala Lumpur. On his thirty-first birthday he caught a Chinese schoolboy slipping pineapple sticks into a satchel. He beat the boy mercilessly in sight of the Malay bank manager, who was on his way back from lunch. The manager offered him an honorable job inside the bank that very afternoon. From that day forth Gurmit's father stood twenty-seven paces from where he had once hawked fruit. He rocked on his heels all day, shaded and cool inside the doorway, dressed in sharp-creased khaki inscribed with the Malayan Banking Corporation logo, stroking the handle of a long truncheon that fell with terrible effect onto the shoulders of malingering Chinese thugs and Malay motorcycle cowboys.

Now retired, the man looked with satisfaction upon the fates of Gurmit's three older brothers, all of whom had received an education and become schoolteachers in the suburbs of Kuala Lumpur. Each had earned the respect of his peers. Each had risen to the post of discipline master for the upper grades. Every morning at the pre-class assemblies they caned the latecomers; at noon they boxed the ears of cheeky Hindu delinquents; in the afternoon they pummeled the shoulders of the sons of malingering Chinese thugs and Malay motorcycle cowboys with reedy switches that sang through the air like hummingbirds.

Gurmit declined to take up the shovel, the truncheon, or the switch. He would not hack at chickens. He would not stomp across the floor to deliver blows. He would not train his ear to gauge the yelps of adversaries, nor lift bowling pins to strengthen his arms. He would, he told his father and brothers, wield the sword of the righteous man. His was the better way, still noble, still the way of the warrior caste. He would wield authority *here* he said, pointing to his head, and *here*, pointing to his heart. His father groaned, and his brothers mocked him behind his back.

But he was not deterred. Bloody hell, he said. Watch me. He read Plato and the German philosophers to strengthen his thoughts. He studied the lives of leaders from Mahatma Gandhi to General Patton to Machiavelli, to clarify his intentions. He joined the Debate Society to focus his speech. He attended the Selangor Club's Men of Tomorrow meetings to hone his ambition. He drank whiskey with women to learn strategy. In time, he distanced himself from his father and brothers. He cropped his hair. He wore rectangular glasses with flexible earpieces. He dressed in safari suits of white cotton. He was gracious and polite to Chinese taxi drivers. He tipped the girls in restaurants, as the British did. He denounced brutality in Hindi musicals. He excoriated the ballsy poetry in Sikh weeklies ("Oh Woman! My fingers / are eight lies about darkness"). He lent money freely and wagged his head suggestively at love songs sung by Freddy Fender. Upon passing his O-level exams and leaving school forever, he took a job shuttling refugees from the Kuala Lumpur transit camp to the airport. One year later he was promoted, after insisting on working at Bidong Island. He would lead, and his leadership would inspire. He would be righteous, and his righteousness would ease the burden of the boat people he read about in the *New Straits Times*.

After a month on the island he was given a small plywood office built on stilts to rise above the monsoon mud. The floor slats had been hurriedly pounded together, and in the gaps he saw the inquisitive, upturned faces of open-mouthed Vietnamese children. When he moved, the faces moved with him. They yammered loudly to their mothers and fathers lounging in their burlap shelters, reporting the dramas unfolding inches above them. From his first day, lines of Vietnamese petitioners, accompanied by self-appointed translators, quietly jammed the steps in the early morning and filed in. In two months he was exhausted. The refugees wore him down with pleading. They softened him with weeping. They enticed him with lascivious bribes. They wanted interviews with Western delegations, for resettlement. They wanted cooking pots in Zone C, running shorts in Zone F. They wanted Mr. Huang removed as Vietnamese chief of Zone A.

Later in the morning the white relief workers would knife through the crowd of petitioners outside his door. Howdy, they would say, and when they did, the children under the floorboards would begin to chatter excitedly. The white people would stand, circling like tigers, or drop with a thud onto the low bench in front of the desk. They told him they weren't there to tell him his job, and they made sure he understood this point by thumping their index fingers on the desktop and staring him straight in the eye. They demanded more rations for the refugees, more plastic tarp, more extensive responsibilities, better lines of communication. They warned that they didn't give a hooey who was running the show, that Task Force chief Ahmed Buttinski, or whatever his name was, better keep his paws off Miss Duong, or Dung, or Jung, they weren't sure how to pronounce it. In the afternoons the Malay Task Force police sauntered in, clothed in sarongs, sometimes with ancient carbines slung across their shoulders. They queried him for information on thieving Chinese Tongs and psychotic ex-ARVN Ranger Scouts and troublemaking white bastards. They frowned at his decision to provide lumber for Zone A while Zone B still needed a supply depot. They derided him for cleaning out the processed chicken in Zone F to give to the new arrivals in Zone C. In the early evening, just as the beaches began to fill with loungers, he would hunch over the wireless to report to the mainland officials. They spoke sharply into his earpiece: Where are the tuberculosis clearance sheets for the Canadian group-*lah?* Why haven't you transferred the burn case to the Kuala Trengganu hospital-*lah?* Why aren't the cabbage baskets on the supply boat-*lah?* Who are you to give a camp pass to the Swedish-whore journalist-*lah?*

By dinner his mind blistered with doubt and worry. He had too much to do, and he made too many mistakes. The Vietnamese manipulated him. The police looked down upon him. The whites walked over him. The UN officials berated him. He was alone. Every day he rose from his desk and threw down a candy sweet to the children gathered under the floor, shuffling the candy over to a gap with his sandal. And every day, opening the door, he found himself surrounded by petitioners. A great cry always went up, and refugees thrust documents in his face. "Later," he said, waving them off, "I'll get to you all. I promise." He walked past the police barracks, and shouted hello to the sleepy-eyed Malays; then he walked down the main footpath and shouted hello to the sullen Vietnamese hunkered in their burlap and plastic huts.

As he walked he thought of food, but he could not eat with the Malay Task Force police because he reported to the UN and MRCS officials on the mainland, not to the Malaysian Prison Systems. And he could not eat with the refugees because they barely had enough to feed themselves. So he walked down to the staff eating hut, where the white people had meals at a huge wooden table covered with a red-and-white checkered plastic tablecloth. "Hellooo, Gurmit!" they said. "How's the paper pusher today?" He smiled, attempting to follow their rapid-fire jokes. He told them his problems and they nodded and pressed him for details about the police and Vietnamese, then patted his back and told him he should get out of the office more because he was in a *refugee camp*, for crying out loud, and the real work, the satisfying stuff, was out among the Viets, not cooped up in that hot box he called an office. The stories started when the last spoonfuls of leftover cuttlefish and rice had been scooped up by the Vietnamese kitchen ladies, who rolled the bits into balls they carried away after clean-up. The teachers related how Mr. Nyouc, a star intermediate-English student, had distracted a guard while they sneaked into the Task Force storehouse to steal notebooks for their classes. The engineers talked about leading lightning raids with their Vietnamese camp-generator team deep into the UN speedboat depot: oil barrel spotted, oil barrel requisitioned, oil barrel *in use*. The social workers revealed they had just that day orchestrated a heist of canned milk for their weaning mothers in Zone F from the black market in Zone C.

The stories made Gurmit weak. Why couldn't they wait? He could make things work, if only he were given the time. He issued feeble protests and was met with withering glares. One day they lectured him in terrifying, unfamiliar tones: "Do you think this is about *paperwork?* There are people out there *in need*. We *have* what they need. We *need* to get it to them. We need to do it *now*."

Gurmit listened politely. He told them he understood, but they must think of the future. They must consider the long-term effects. Establish order first. Go slow and steady, for if they didn't mind him telling them so, Task Force and Doctor Johansson in Kuala Trengganu and even the director of UNV and the subofficers of UNHCR thought the camp staff too—well, yes, he would say it—too independent.

"That's very Asian," said the teacher.

The social worker pointed out that Asians had a much different sense of time than westerners were used to. The engineer asked if Kronos were a Hindu god, or just Greek.

"I am a Sikh," said Gurmit. "I am not Hindu."

"So where's your turban?" asked the engineer.

"Bullshit," said the teacher. "Sikhs don't wear turbans."

"I thought they carried knives," said the social worker. She asked Gurmit if he carried a knife. Her face was furrowed with worry.

Bloody hell, thought Gurmit. He plucked his fork off his plate and brandished it like a stiletto, waving it in the air. He decided to keep his problems to himself.

After dinner, he often returned to his office to complete refugee arrival forms. He found solace in the deserted office, after the refugees had to leave the administrative compound. A fluorescent tube burned over his head, and geckos slithered out from the wall slats to feast on mosquitoes and moths. He would lean back, listening to Vietnamese music screeching from the loudspeakers. Relax, he thought. Concentrate on the task at hand. Despair is for cowards. For assurance, he would stare at the glossy sheet above the door-jamb, where he had hammered an advertisement from an *India Today!* magazine. The caption at the bottom read "Captain Knows Best. We Sail, You Rest." Above it was a color photo of a human V-wedge, men and women arranged like migrating birds. At the ends were black cooks in starched high hats, and beaming brown stewards. In the middle danced a conga line of busty white women with golden hair that fell on their shoulders like shocks of wheat. Their arms were wrapped around Teutonic men in creased tropical shirts. At the front, where he belonged, stood a strapping, cropped-hair Sikh in naval attire. The picture invigorated Gurmit. The island inhabitants were not yet that disciplined V-wedge. The refugees were not yet those casual, secure travelers. The staff was not yet those steady, contented workers. And he was not yet that strapping, cropped-hair Sikh captain. But he would be. In his heart he knew he would. He would be the invisible hand steering the course. He would be the righteous leader.

In preparation for that day, he had placed a dignified white and black naval hat in his bottom desk drawer. When that day came — when order reigned — he would take the hat from his drawer, place it on his head, and parade around the camp. He would wear it to lunch. He would wear it on the dock when he stood to greet the UN delegations. The Malays and the refugees would not think it odd. They would envy his dry head during the monsoons.

No one would say anything at first. But then the white people would begin to bellow their hellos from the beach and the class-rooms and the incinerator, and raise imaginary hats in greeting. They would laugh at first, but the fact that he wore the cap would be in their minds. Soon a group of whites would smile hugely when Gurmit, still in his cap, walked past the staff bungalows. "Gurmit, up here," one would say, and Gurmit would stride up the steps. A bottle of Johnnie Walker Black Label would appear, and one of the men would pour him a glass with a great show of stealth, overdra-matizing the danger that the Task Force police, Muslims all, would enforce the silly no-liquor rule.

The palaver would start. First his host would yell down to a fa-vorite refugee across the wire fence, an English speaker, probably some ravaged ex-bargirl with bad teeth. "Keep an eye out for the police," his host would say to the girl. "We're having a snort." And the girl would smile and yell back "Okay, Mr. Bob," or Mr. Tom, or Mr. Dennis—it really made little difference who spoke, as long as the face was white—and having smiled and waved theatrically, the girl would make a grand show of carrying out her duties and bark out commands to a dozen nephews and sisters, who would fan out like miniature snipers, keeping low in the shadows, in full sight of the white man, and watch for some passing, sarong-clad Malay policeman on his way to the police bathing well. The white man would watch until his sentries were in position, and the play would draw to its final scene. The white man would wink to the girl, and the girl would giggle. He would pause, look out at the sky, then focus on Gurmit and raise his glass. Their glasses would meet and clink. The white man would raise an imaginary hat with his free hand and say, "Cheers, Captain."

When that moment came, Gurmit knew, all the white people would call him Captain, for the white people spoke with one voice. In a few more days the Malay police would also call him Captain, for the Malays feared the language of the white bastards and made it their own whenever they could. And then the Vietnamese would call him Captain, for the white people and the Malays spoke the language of power. All would call him Captain, for that is what he would be. All would see he had brought order. All would see the camp running well, the supplies in place, rations increased, the delegations whisking in and whisking out, the hospital finished, another school in Zone B. They would eat together, Malays and whites; the concertina wire would be torn from the police and staff compound and shipped to the mainland; and the refugees would squat contentedly in their huts, awaiting their orderly procession onto the idling UN boats, where they would sit in comfort and look out over the ocean, drawing ever closer to places where they would not disappear, name and body and life.

"You're in a refugee camp, little bugger." The words, spoken by the British engineer, still stung in Gurmit's ears. Bloody hell, of course he was in a refugee camp. That was why he wanted to leave. And why he now marched down the Zone C footpath with a damaged wooden plank from the staff eating hut. He carried it like a surf-board, under his armpit, striding purposefully back to his office. Behind him, his new Vietnamese administrative assistant, Miss Phu from Zone F, jogged to keep up. He spat. Of all things to carry, a table plank. He would just as soon tack one of the red-and-white checkered plastic tablecloths over it and go about his business. But that British engineer! How dare he. The man's words had left Gurmit with little choice. He was, in any event, legally justified in taking the board, for the operating orders of the Malaysian Prison Systems were quite specific: "Destruction of government property shall be reported to the administrative chief, who shall initiate a full inves-tigation to determine culpability if the persons and causes respon-sible are not known." So that was just what he would do. The damaged plank from the staff eating table, property of the Malay-sian Prison Systems, was now in his charge, to remain in his office until such time as the investigation was complete. Let the staff complain all they wanted.

The refugees on the footpath cleared out of his way. Miss Phu, unable to match his pace, weaved from side to side to avoid being struck by the bobbing plank and explained as well as she could to curious pedestrians what Gurmit was carrying. Overhead, the slate-gray sky rumbled. A light rain began to fall.

"Mr. Gurmit, you walk so fast," Miss Phu said. She held his clipboard with both hands, like a serving tray.

"Bloody hell," he said sharply. "Are we having a picnic? Come."

Miss Phu detected his impatience and loped after him, shifting the clipboard to her left in anticipation of Gurmit's wide turn. "Wah!" she giggled. "No picnic. Too much rain."

Gurmit cocked his head to the side and shouted over a list of new announcements issuing from the loudspeaker. "This is *Sikh* rain. You see?" He looked down at his white safari suit, now mottled with drops.

"Not sick, Mr. Gurmit."

Gurmit sighed. Why could he never get assistants who spoke good English? Since the beginning of the rains last week he and Miss Phu had established a code that allowed them to carry out business in secret: complaints from Vietnamese were yellow rain; from the Malay police, brown rain; from the staff, white rain. The least she could do was understand Sikh rain.

"No," he shouted back. "*Sikh*. Indian Sikh, like me. This is *my* rain. I'm complaining."

"Ahhh," shouted Miss Phu. "Very funny, Mr. Gurmit."

Gurmit had not meant it as a joke. Just minutes ago, his daily status meeting in the eating hut had dissolved into Sikh rain. The evidence under his arm had been just another plank in the table. The insulting British engineer had been just another relief worker. How could things have gone bad so quickly? He gave the board a whack against a palm tree by the joss-stick sellers. For two months he had wolfed down lunch and dinner in the eating hut, his roving fork just inches away from the gouges in the plank. He had thought nothing of the wood's imperfections because the table was always covered with a red-and-white checkered plastic tablecloth held down with tacks. He and the staff all ate their cuttlefish and rice on plastic plates, resting their elbows on the greasy red-and-white covering. Occasionally someone would spill coffee or water, and when the liquid gathered in pools on the plank now tucked firmly under his arm, they simply moved their plates.

But when, at the conclusion of that morning's status meeting, Bobbi Sortini knocked over her tea, Gurmit noticed something peculiar. He saw the liquid arrange itself in the form of letters. He made out a *T*, an *N*, and possibly an *H*. He put his fingers on the thick plastic covering and pressed so hard the tablecloth pulled against the tacks holding it. He announced that the gouges seemed to be letters.

"Alphabet soup!" cried the radiologist.

"Spelling Bee!" said the British engineer.

Gurmit and the radiologist began to push the water jugs and coffee cups to one side to make room for their investigation. As they did, Miss Thi, the head of the Vietnamese kitchen ladies, began to bustle around them and move the water jugs and coffee cups back to their original positions. She snapped at her two assistants, who ran from the cooking fire behind the corrugated tin wall, and the three of them scurried to put metal cups over the center of the table. Gurmit and the radiologist drew back in surprise.

"What's wrong, Miss Thi?" asked Bobbi, lingering at the entrance. She cast a sharp look at Gurmit and the radiologist and, placing her arm around her friend Miss Thi, drew out from the woman that the grooves did indeed spell something. Miss Thi swore she had nothing to do with it. "It's okay, Miss Thi," said Bobbi. "No problem." Gurmit smiled and nodded. "No problem," said the radiologist.

Miss Thi appeared relieved. Speaking in Vietnamese, she told her assistants to unroll the window tarp so no passersby could see in. At the same time, Miss Thi helped Gurmit and the radiologist strip the tacks from the tablecloth. When they finished, they peeled off the covering and with much effort tossed the stiff plastic onto the dirt floor. There before them they saw the words *Nguyen Van Trinh* in perfectly carved letters almost half a foot high.

"That name," said Gurmit.

"The suicide, isn't he?" said Bobbi, pointing.

"That right," said Miss Thi. "That right. That right. I not do the cut. I not know who do the cut."

"That's okay, Miss Thi," said Bobbi. She held Miss Thi's hand. "No one's blaming you. No problem. Gurmit buried him, didn't you Gurmit? If anyone knows who did this, Gurmit does."

"Did not," said Gurmit quickly.

"Meaning?" said Bobbi.

"Did not bury." He shook his head violently. "I am only signing paperwork, isn't it? Did not bury. Health division is responsible to bury. You understand-*lah*? I did not bury."

"All right, already," said Bobbi.

"Only signing paperwork. You understand, yes? Other people are burying, isn't it?"

"So who was he?" said the mechanic from Colorado.

"I'm afraid no one really knows," said Bobbi. "A name. The meta-refugee."

The British engineer chuckled. "Here's something, mates. Bet you buggers have never seen this." He reached into his pocket and pulled out a lighter. Unscrewing the bottom, he held it over the table and poured lighter fluid into one of the gouges. Pointing to the lightness of the stain, he pronounced the cutting to have taken place about a month ago.

The radiologist shook his head. He produced a curled shaving. "Much too supple," he said, squeezing it with his fingers. He believed it no more than a week old.

The mechanic from Colorado disputed both claims. "Over here," he said, and he pressed Bobbi's hands into the grooves, letting her feel the texture of the grain. "See how smooth? That's a year old if it's a day."

"The cut *always* been there," said Miss Thi suddenly.

"Just poof, huh?" said the engineer. "Abacadabara."

"Always there," Miss Thi said. She hiccupped.

"Magic," said the engineer. "The Ur-cut."

"Okay, then," said the radiologist. "The inexplicable. Who am I to argue?"

"Please," said Gurmit. "No more. You're upsetting Miss Thi."

"Yes, holy one," said the engineer. He salaamed in Gurmit's direction.

"You are making fun," Gurmit said.

The engineer raised his eyebrows. "I'm pointing out you're taking the high road again."

"I am not understanding why you say this," said Gurmit.

"Forget it," said the engineer.

"I'm telling you this is upsetting Miss Thi," said Gurmit.

"You're the one continuing this," said the engineer. "Look who's upsetting Miss Thi now." He pointed at her.

"Always there," Miss Thi said, then brought her hands to her face.

"Will you two shut up," said Bobbi.

"I am not taking the high road," said Gurmit. "If I am taking, then my job is to make an investigation." He pointed to the plank. "Find who has committed this crime, yes? But I am not doing. Do you see an investigation?"

"Come on, cowboys," said the radiologist. "Time to saddle up and skedaddle." He stood at the entrance.

"What are you saying?" said Gurmit. "I am not watching cowboys and Indians. What are you saying?"

"He's not saying anything," said the engineer. "Good God Almighty. I thought *Brits* were supposed to be uptight."

"So Malaysians are uptight," said Gurmit.

"It was you I had more in mind," said the engineer.

"I'm sorry you think so. You say anything you want, isn't it?"

"You need a paperwork fix, mate. I'm sorry I came to the meeting at all."

"Please take this outside," said Bobbi.

"And now the meeting is silly," said Gurmit.

"You're in a *refugee camp*, little bugger," said the engineer. "Think about it."

Gurmit began to click his pen rapidly. "Is that where I am?" he said. He felt everyone's eyes on him. He heard someone snigger. "A refugee camp, hey?" he said.

"Oh, don't get angry," said Bobbi.

"I am in a refugee camp," Gurmit snapped. He moved quickly. He lifted the plank and placed it under his arm. "Then I am administration chief, isn't it? I am keeping this damaged property for evidence." He clutched his clipboard with his free hand and stepped outside. The board nearly rammed Miss Phu, who was on her way to his office.

Late that night Gurmit sat hunched over his typewriter, staring at the words he had just typed onto his Preliminary Damage Report sheet. Against the wall leaned the plank, and there it would stay. That name. He could not bring himself to look at the gouges. Had he not finished with Nguyen Van Trinh? A most unpleasant business. But he could not simply be done with it by returning the table plank to its rightful place. Just thinking about the consequences made his heart race. If he walked back to the eating hut with the plank, a crowd of Viets would follow. They would pester Miss Phu for information, and Miss Phu would say she didn't know why he was returning the plank. But, she would add, he had been angry when he brought it to his office. Ah, the crowd would say, and then they would rush into the hospital and the administrative offices to drag out English-speaking relatives who worked with the white people. The relatives would seek out Bobbi Sortini and the British engineer and ask why Mr. Gurmit was angry with them.

"Well," the engineer would say, "he's a twit."

"Well," Bobbi would say, "he's upset that he can't do his job."

"Ah," the relatives would say, smiling. "Poor Mr. Gurmit."

The relatives would ruin him. At night, when the generator shuddered to a stop, the refugees would squat by their cardboard beds and drink warm tea. The relatives would tell the story of Mr. Gurmit and the plank. They would say he had been angry with the white people. He had been defeated. He was a twit Indian, an angry Indian. The words would hang in the air. In the morning, when Gurmit opened his office door, the children under the floorboards would call up and greet him. They would think his name had changed: Angry Mr. Gurmit, they would say, repeating the words they had heard. Twit Mr. Gurmit. Poor Mr. Gurmit. They would repeat the words over and over, not even knowing their meanings, and then Task Force Chief Ahmed would walk up the steps and open the door to tell him what he could not bear to hear: Gurmit, Ahmed would say, the white bastards are playing you for the fool.

Unbearable. He had to carry through with an investigation—at least the pretense of one. For if the plank-gouger were discovered . . . It was painful to contemplate. Task Force guards would take a rattan to the culprit and shave his head and lock him inside the chicken coop for days. Gurmit shook his head violently, driving the images away. He would employ all of his advantages over the Vietnamese to prevent discovery from occurring. Surely his advantages would be sufficient. Typing his name at the bottom of the report, he reviewed them once again. He signed the delegation interview request forms. He assigned ration allotments and allocated clothing supplies to the zone chiefs. All the Viets knew that. And surely no Viet would challenge his authority to refuse information regarding the culprit, or to bury it under mounds of paper. They understood how power worked. Silence was assured.

But there was still delicate work ahead. Island operating orders

required four signatures on the Preliminary Damage Report sheet—
his own and those representing the three groups on the island: the
Malaysian Task Force chief, Ahmed; the Vietnamese zone chief of
the area in which the crime occurred, Mr. Cho; and the senior UN
staff member, Bobbi Sortini. He drummed his index finger on the
space bar. Well, he had certain advantages in dealing with the
Malays and the white people too. He assuredly did. He cracked his
knuckles. Yes. An investigation could be made to fail. He ripped
the sheet from the typewriter and secured it to his clipboard. The
words looked bold and formidable. He nodded with satisfaction
and, after walking briskly to his bungalow, crawled into bed immediately and fell asleep.

The next morning Gurmit tacked a sign on his office door announc-
ing in three languages he would be out for the morning. From his
hand hung the clipboard containing his Preliminary Damage Report. Marching down the footpath, he could not help but stop
several times to reread what he had written. "One table plank, Malaysian Red Crescent property (value: 5 ringgit), damaged; investigation initiated for purposes of determining cause and/or responsibility, per operating orders." His breath was labored. The words
now seemed so thin, so inadequate. The type was smudged. There
was an unsightly crusted spot of Wite-Out by his name. He admitted to himself he was feeling neither confident nor confrontational.
But he recalled the words of the great Sikh warrior Murthabi Singh:
Praise the day you meet your enemy, for on that day you shall become a hero. The words of the great Murthabi Singh calmed him.
His safari suit pocket bristled with pens; the clipboard settled
squarely against his breast. He praised the day.

He spotted Task Force Chief Ahmed seated on a stool under a
coconut tree near the Zone D beach. In attendance was a Vietnamese barber reputed to have cut the hair of American officers at

Da Nang. The barber, outfitted in large black running shorts, held a pair of scissors and a plastic comb. Ahmed stared into a handmirror and directed the barber by signaling with his free hand. Outside the dry bubble under the tree, a small rain began and punched tiny holes in the sand.

The moment seemed propitious. Ahmed, normally a little jittery, sat relaxed, looking out at the long sheets of water lapping onto shore. He had run to fat in the way of Malay men: a graceful, tiny frame erupting in the middle, as if an epidermic seal had broken and organs surged against his shirt. Gurmit studied Ahmed's face. The man stared off into the water, blinking when the barber snipped around his ears, contemplative even, expectant, like a man scanning a bookshelf for a title. Gurmit felt he understood him as well as he understood anyone on the island. The Task Force chief often passed around a creased picture of his eight children and wife Hanisah, whose eyes, Gurmit thought, were as puffy and hooded as a lizard's. Did he beat her? Gurmit wondered. As a family man, he probably did. But Ahmed believed in order, and in that respect Gurmit felt he and the Task Force chief had much in common. Yet the man was corrupt, there was no denying it, and in talking to him, Gurmit sometimes sensed a reserve from the police chief, a preoccupation, as if conversation were a task to be performed, a kind of public duty one carried out until the door could be closed and the clothes stripped off. In Ahmed's office was a small stack of sweetened milk and bags of potatoes—refugee supplies. Once, Gurmit had seen a Viet longshoreman open Ahmed's office door and dump a box onto the floor.

"This is Bidong Island," Ahmed said one day, reviewing population figures with Gurmit. Ahmed had smiled at Gurmit's notice of the boxes and burlap sacks in the corner. "I give these to my friends," Ahmed said. "Here friend. Have some *susu* for your coffee." And then he reached down and tossed Gurmit a can of sweetened condensed milk. Gurmit caught it and tucked it into his safari-jacket pocket.

Under the tree, Ahmed did not receive Gurmit's news well. "So now someone is damaging tables?" He made a kissing noise. "So what to do?" Ahmed said. "What? I have only twenty-five men here to keep peace among . . . *apa?*" He snapped his fingers and rolled his eyes skyward to secure the number. "Among 28,462 Vietnamese, and this butcher here." He turned his head slightly to indicate the barber, who deftly drew back his barbering instruments, like a surgeon wielding a scalpel. "Therefore," continued Ahmed, wagging his finger at Gurmit, "I cannot keep watch over the white bastards' table."

"No, no," said Gurmit. "I am not questioning security procedures. I am reporting only what has occurred. But in point of fact, is not 28,463 Vietnamese. This is my job, you know, and I am quite certain that you are in error."

"No. *Tidak,*" said Ahmed, shaking his head. "28,463."

"You will recall," said Gurmit, "we are sending eighty-one ethnic Chinese to Kuala Lumpur last Tuesday, and you are forgetting the four fishermen, we presume drowned, who have stolen the Zone F blackboard to build their boat."

"Yes-*lah,*" nodded Ahmed. "I will subtract eighty-five from my figure, but you must keep in mind three things. Our flame-thrower has not yet arrived. Our m-16s from America are still in Kuala Trengganu with white bastard Mr. Thomas. Our grenade launcher does not have a pin. And one more thing, my friend—*apa?* that is four—six-hundred meters of concertina wire have been diverted to Pulau Rendah."

"So is not 28,463," said Gurmit.

"Yes, but you are not listening to what I am saying," said Ahmed. He turned his attention to the barber, directing him to an uneven tuft by his left ear.

Gurmit examined the barber's handiwork. "Some here, too," Gurmit said, tapping Ahmed's crown. Ahmed furrowed his brow and peered closely into the mirror.

"Security," said Gurmit suddenly, "is not my job, but I am thinking the damaged table is only the eyes of the crocodile. Zone A has had so many fights this month, yes? I have seen with my own eyes. I sleep better at night when I see so many police." Gurmit held forth his clipboard. "I will tell police commander Zainal of my concern when I talk to him next."

"Oh-*lah!*" said Ahmed, laughing. "Is a bribe, yes? You are giving a bribe." He held his hand out and rubbed his fingers together.

"No bribe," said Gurmit.

"Butcher, you hear that? Mr. Gurmit will tell Zainal of my concern. But no bribe."

The barber held his scissors aloft and smiled.

"No bribe," said Gurmit.

"No bribe," said Ahmed, giggling into his shirt. The barber quickly snipped at the hairs on his nape. "Gurmit, we will make a policeman of you yet."

For a moment the three men were silent. The barber snipped quickly around Ahmed's left ear, straightening to hear the heave-ho yells coming up from the Zone F beach, where a line of men strained on a chain to pull out an engine block buried in the sand. Gurmit wagged his clipboard in front of Ahmed's handmirror.

"I am needing your signature," said Gurmit, withdrawing a pen from his breast pocket.

Ahmed took the clipboard and Gurmit watched him read, following the police chief's eyes. Ahmed began humming. He nodded as he read, and each time his head shifted, the barber let out small cries and drew the scissors away. "I see," said Ahmed. He held the clipboard out for Gurmit to take.

"Can sign?" said Gurmit, refusing the item.

"Can sign," Ahmed said. "If."

"If?"

"If-*lah*. Can sign, if-*lah*." He waved his hand in the barber's face. "Butcher. *Ooi*." The barber frowned and raised his scissors again, snipping the air, as Ahmed leaned forward and reached into his back pocket. He extracted a worn manila envelope, folded in two.

"For better sleeping," he said. He opened it. A huge grin spread over his face.

Inside were black-and-white photos of nude Vietnamese women, some glumly splaying their legs, others kneeling with their buttocks aimed at the camera. In the background were the metal bunk frames found in the Task Force barracks.

The barber, snipping vaguely in Ahmed's direction, sidled up and looked with interest over Gurmit's shoulder. Gurmit chased the man back with loud hisses. His teeth were bared.

Ahmed eyed Gurmit closely. "Come on-*lah*," he said. "You like girls, yes? Keep for a few days. Forget your troubles, yes?"

Gurmit raised his eyebrows. He stood motionless, his pen poised over the clipboard, looking over at the men straining to pull the engine from the sand. His fingers trembled.

"You can sign?" Gurmit said.

"You can take?" said Ahmed, holding out the envelope.

Gurmit took it. He handed the clipboard to Ahmed.

Ahmed put down the handmirror and grinned. Gurmit tapped the signatory line several times with his finger.

"Yes, yes," Ahmed said, and took the pen from Gurmit's hand. "Keep for a few days-*lah*," he said, nodding toward the envelope. "Think sweeter thoughts."

Gurmit watched Ahmed put pen to paper. The man's looping signature looked like nothing Gurmit had imagined. There was a scrawl along the signatory line, then airy, soaring circles above, as if the letters were detaching from themselves.

"If I catch the culprit," Gurmit said, surprising himself with the passion in his voice, "my thoughts will be sweet as rambutan fruit. This table. Very upsetting, isn't it?"

Ahmed made a sucking sound. The barber stopped to see if he had nicked the man's ear. "Rambutan!" said Ahmed. "Sweet as dreams, yes?" His face blossomed.

Gurmit closed his eyes, pretending he didn't hear. He tucked the manila envelope into his pocket. He made a check by Ahmed's name and marched up the main footpath to find Mr. Cho, the Vietnamese Zone D chief.

Gurmit felt a breeze, and the sensation made him worry he was naked. He was stepping over the bobbing plank that served as a bridge over the Zone D sewer canal. He almost fell. Bloody hell, he thought: pictures. He could not believe he had not known of their existence. He could not believe Ahmed had carried them so casually, like a wallet. He slipped his hand under his safari jacket and pushed the envelope farther down in his pocket. The plank wobbled behind him. The ground felt secure under his feet. He stopped. The air was filled with odor: moist human wastes, diesel fuel, wet cardboard. A small boy nearby buzzed on the end of a tightly wound palm frond, and in the sound, Gurmit heard a roar.

He wound his way through Zone D, stepping over buckets, skirting mud, repeating to himself the words of the great Murthabi Singh. He praised the day, his lips moving to the words in his head. Outside Cho's shelter a woman held an umbrella of palm leaves over her head. In her other hand, she bore a foot-long lizard corpse, swinging stiffly from a length of pink yarn. Gurmit straightened his jacket and wiped the tiny drops of rain from his head.

He pulled aside Cho's flour-sack door and found the zone chief squatting on the smooth dirt floor, occupied with making a hat for his young son from an empty Marlboro carton. The boy retreated into the darkness, past a corrugated tin sheet in the back.

"Ah," said Cho, rising.

The zone chief was barechested, dressed only in black running shorts and flip-flops. He motioned for Gurmit to sit on the tree stump opposite him. This Gurmit did, kicking the stump with the soles of his sandals to remove the mud. Cho pushed aside the flour-sack doorway to give Gurmit light to clean by. Then the flour sack dropped back over the entrance, and the hut darkened. Daylight illuminated the cloth, creating a screen the two men could look through while not being seen from the outside. When Gurmit raised his head in acknowledgment of Cho's gesture, he saw figures walking along the footpath, their outlines shadowy as ghosts.

For a refugee, Cho could be difficult. He was the former Tae Kwan Do champion of Quang Ngan. As a young man, he had told Gurmit, he could break two inches of oak, or six inches of ice, or five inches of sandstone, all with thrusts of his feet. With his head, he could break four inches of double-ply palm wood, or seven inches of ice. That had been years ago, though his arms were still latticed with sinew. On Bidong Island he spent his days combing his long hair with a pink styling comb bought from a Malay trader and practicing his English. He walked with the tight gait of the permanently angry, for he had been rich in Vietnam, a colonel in the army, and after five years in re-education camps he emerged with his health broken—his hair was thinning and white—and his bean plantation turned into a tire factory. As Gurmit well knew, he had elected himself to his zone chief position, although other Vietnamese were more qualified. But since none of the refugees wanted trouble with him, they let him have his way. His mind was forever full of tricks, and Gurmit imagined that even his two children had been the result of diplomatic maneuvering with his ruddy-skinned wife, who never seemed to lack for rice or tea.

Cho received the news about the plank much more calmly than Ahmed had. He squatted across from Gurmit, nodding thoughtfully. "Tea," he said to his wife, in English. Gurmit peered into the darkness and noticed the woman behind a corrugated tin divider, squatting over a pot that lay on a circle of blackened charcoal. "I not know the criminal," said Cho, returning his attention to Gurmit. "But I can help you find who is the one."

"At this point," said Gurmit, quickly, "I wish simply to inform all parties and receive their signatures." He held up his clipboard for Cho to examine, pointing to the line where his signature would go. "At a later date I will contact you if we need help."

"Tea," said Cho again to his wife. The woman looked up, smiling at Gurmit, and appeared to address someone—the boy, Gurmit assumed—behind the corrugated tin, where they kept supplies.

Cho snapped at his wife in Vietnamese, then turned his attention again to Gurmit. "I understand your meaning, Mr. Gurmit," he said. "At a later date you *may* ask me."

Gurmit shook his head. It was sad, in a way. Cho wished to establish complicity: two men reading between the lines. How disappointed Cho would be when he realized there was nothing of the sort to read. "My meaning is clear," said Gurmit. "I will ask you at a later date."

"Yes, *will* ask," said Cho. "You know, I have a difficult time to hear with the loudspeaker. All the time so much noise." He swept his arm back and forth in a wide arc, as if sweeping the air clean of sound. Gurmit listened to the sing-song loudspeaker voices listing boat departure numbers.

"Departure list so boring," said Cho. "I like the music better. In the morning yesterday they play Vietnamese song. Do you like?"

"I like."

"Ah! You can say this to Mr. Tan in loudspeaker division. Vietnamese song number one."

"Mr. Cho," said Gurmit, "the loudspeaker division is not my job. *You* tell them. I am not caring what they play."

"You say you like Vietnamese song, Mr. Gurmit. Just now you say it."

Gurmit waved his hand. "I am not telling anyone what song to play," he said. He imagined Tan's pinched face screwing up in disagreement at his request.

"Something wrong here, Mr. Gurmit," said Cho. He placed his hands on his knees and began to rock on the balls of his feet.

Gurmit grew alarmed at Cho's remark. Had the pictures fallen out? Pretending to scratch his back, he felt his back pocket for the manila envelope. It was there. He grew irritated: if Cho wanted to play games, he had chosen the wrong partner.

"I am happy to see you so comfortable," said Gurmit, mimicking Cho's rocking.

"I am thinking of Vietnamese song."

"One thing," said Gurmit, holding up a finger. "If you are liking, tell the loudspeaker division. I will not. That is not why I have come to see you."

"Something wrong here, Mr. Gurmit," said Cho, his voice flat.

"What do you mean?" said Gurmit. He leaned forward to examine Cho's expression. "You are always saying this. Zone D is always having problems."

"No, no," said Cho, shaking his head. "Not every time."

"Oh yes," said Gurmit, rising. "Every time. 'Something wrong here.' That is all you say. You have said it about the cut cable lines—it was your Mr. Dong, you know—and the missing running shorts. What is wrong here now? What do you mean?" Gurmit waved the clipboard in Cho's face.

"Mr. Gurmit, I can hear informations about the table," said Cho. "But every day, loudspeakers hurt my ears." He pressed his hands to his ears.

"Ah, so that is it," said Gurmit. "I scratch yours, you scratch mine, hey? I repeat. I am not telling the loudspeaker division. I am not interested in your information. I am wanting you to sign. That is all." He sat down again, thrusting the clipboard at Cho with one hand and pulling out his pen with the other.

"Oh, but Mr. Gurmit," said Cho, taking the clipboard and pen. "I have a difficult time to find informations for you with so much noise." He then did an astonishing thing. He withdrew his pink styling comb from the band in his running shorts and pulled it through his hair. His eyes roamed over Gurmit's safari suit.

The sight was unnerving. Combing his hair! Leering! It wasn't refugee behavior, not in front of a staff person. Confused, Gurmit looked down at his clipboard and pretended to read. Then he understood. Cho was flaunting his power. He commanded the eyes and ears of Zone D, and he would open them only if Gurmit talked to

Mr. Tan. Gurmit smiled in sympathy. The zone chief just didn't get it. There the man was, pulling a pink comb through his hair, threatening to withhold information Gurmit did not want. He towered over the zone chief. He sat comfortably on the tree stump. He wore a white suit and carried a clipboard and slept with burning mosquito coils under his bunk. Cho was trying to intimidate the wrong man.

"Mr. Cho," said Gurmit, wearily. "What if I am not caring for your information?"

Cho placed his hands on his knees and left the comb in his hair. "My informations are good. I am zone chief," he said.

"Just so," said Gurmit. "But I am quite busy, you know. Many things can come up. Maybe I am not in such a hurry for information."

"I keep for you here," said Cho, pointing to his head. "I am a bank."

"Yes, yes," said Gurmit. "What I want to say is that other things come up, you know."

"Ah," said Cho. "Many more important things. I understand."

"That is my meaning," said Gurmit.

"I can give informations to Mr. Ahmed," said Cho.

"Is not necessary. He is not caring."

"I can give to someone else," said Cho.

"No," said Gurmit, firmly. "We must follow procedure. I must have your signature to get a chop." He brought his fist down lightly on his knee, imitating the imprinting of the official government seal that would soon appear on the report.

"Yes, chop," said Cho, mimicking Gurmit's action. "Cannot give informations to someone else. Must only sign, yes?"

"Yes, Mr. Cho," said Gurmit. "So sign please." Gurmit pointed to the clipboard and pen still lying across Cho's knees.

Cho looked down at the clipboard. "Something wrong if I tell someone else?"

"No, not something wrong," said Gurmit. "Must have a chop." He again brought his fist down lightly on his knee.

"Maybe," said Cho, plucking the comb from his hair, "something wrong with your report, Mr. Gurmit?" Cho paused, then looked at Gurmit expectantly: eyebrows raised, lips pursed, eyes steady. He began to rock on his feet again.

Gurmit brought his hands to his face and pulled at the skin on his cheeks. *Something wrong with your report?* Cho's expression was frozen. Like a gambler, Gurmit thought. Like a man who has just turned over his card. Cho could send his eyes and ears through the camp. He could talk to Miss Phu. To Ahmed. To Bobbi Sortini. He could make sure they all heard about Mr. Gurmit's morning visit. He could tell them Mr. Gurmit hadn't wanted to know who mutilated the plank. And if Cho did that . . . if Cho did that, Gurmit knew, it was possible, it was assuredly possible, they would all discover the investigation to be a sham, buried beneath a mountain of paper.

Bloody, bloody hell.

Gurmit wiped his face. "Well," he said, "I am thinking you cannot find out the information I want. So mysterious, this table damage. So many people to talk to."

"Mr. Gurmit!" said Cho, wrinkling his forehead. "I am Cho!" He placed his hands over his heart, holding the comb out like a serrated digit. "I can find out many informations."

"Yes," said Gurmit. "Very well. I will make your thinking easier. When I see Mr. Tan of the loudspeaker division, I will tell him of your wish for Vietnamese songs."

"Ah! Something wrong before, now nothing wrong, Mr. Gurmit," said Cho. "My ears hear informations much better with Vietnamese songs. Thank you, Mr. Gurmit. Now, please, I must sign your report." He held out his hand for the clipboard and pen. "Tea, please?" he said.

Gurmit nodded. He felt for a moment that he had never hated anyone more in his life than this man. Squatting, Cho called out in Vietnamese to his wife, still sitting quietly behind the corrugated divider, and she barked back sharply, then entered with warm tea in a cut-off 7-Up can. Gurmit feigned a smile. He plucked out ashes floating on the surface of his can. He looked through a gap between the plastic tarp and the branch frame and saw small rivulets of rain slide down to the dirt floor. The envelope inside his pants cushioned the tree stump. When he shifted his weight, the pictures fanned out under him. They were soft. They were soft like defeat was soft. They were soft like the pillow you sat on when you were defeated, when you sat in the victor's tent and offered your head. How much better the hard surface of the stump!

There was commotion outside. The shadows outlined against the flour-sack door had moved close, large as bears. Their feet were visible. Gurmit saw their arms move. The men outside were eavesdropping. "Huy!" said Gurmit, swatting the cloth. He saw the feet shuffle a bit. Cho looked up. "Huy!" said Gurmit again. The figures held their ground.

Cho then barked something in Vietnamese. The figures answered, compliant, and then just like that, they were gone.

It was humiliating. He, the administration chief, dressed in a white safari suit, was unable even to chase away eavesdroppers. Cho smiled. Gurmit hit the flour sack in return. His head was burning, his stomach knotted. He sipped his tea noisily, watching Cho scribble furiously back and forth across the clipboard.

"No ink, Mr. Gurmit," said Cho. He held up the failed pen to his wife, who called out to their son. The boy knocked what sounded like pots onto the dirt, then entered from behind the divider. He held a red felt pen. Gurmit saw the boy's T-shirt and jumped to his feet, enraged and joyous.

"Bloody hell," he said. He almost sang the words. "Where did you get that T-shirt?" Cho turned and considered his son. The boy's T-shirt read *I Saw the Pope on Bidong Island*. Under the legend was a line drawing of a boat in rough water being towed to clearer water by a motorized shepherd's cane.

"I not stole," said Cho. "Miss Bobbi gives it to me."

Gurmit shook his head. "This T-shirt belongs in Supply."

"I not stole it," repeated Cho. "Miss Bobbi gives me."

"Miss Bobbi or not," said Gurmit, "you are knowing the rules."

"I am not the thief," said Cho.

"We will see if Task Force agrees," said Gurmit. "I hope they do not *bam-bam* you on the head. Be assured I will tell them you are a good man."

Gurmit rose. He brought his finger down hard on the report form. "Sign," he said.

Cho frowned. As he wrote, his hand trembled slightly.

"The T-shirt," said Gurmit, pointing at the boy. Cho spoke to his wife, who then said something hurriedly to their son and shucked the T-shirt over the boy's head. Cho took the cloth from her and put it on top of the clipboard. He held them out like gifts, bowing slightly. "Please," he said, giggling. "For you, please."

Gurmit took them and slowly turned around, one hand on the flour-sack door.

"More tea, please?" said Mr. Cho. "You want more tea?"

Gurmit turned again. "No tea, Mr. Cho," said Gurmit. "I tell you again. You cannot take the T-shirt. Supply will deliver. You cannot take. Cannot. Do you hear? Can. Not. Take." He grabbed a corner of the T-shirt and stuffed it under his belt.

Cho's voice rose sharply: "Did not take, Mr. Gurmit. Did not take."

Gurmit raised his hand. "Oh, maybe I am overreacting, Mr. Cho. This loudspeaker racket, you know? It gives me a headache, too. Oh, and I know how is Miss Bobbi. So very difficult to refuse. So why tell Ahmed, hey?"

"Yes, Mr. Gurmit."

"No need to tell, hey?"

"Yes, Mr. Gurmit."

"Okay-*lah*," said Gurmit. "I will not tell Ahmed."

"Thank you, Mr. Gurmit," said Cho, smiling broadly.

"If I see Tan I will tell him about the music," said Gurmit, placing his hand on Cho's shoulder. "If. He is so busy these days, isn't it? I hate to disturb."

Cho nodded.

"Perhaps it is impossible to talk to him, isn't it?"

"Yes, Mr. Gurmit."

"And I will ask you when I want information about the table, yes, Mr. Cho?" said Gurmit. "I will ask first, isn't it? If I do not ask, I do not want. If I do not want, you do not tell."

Cho nodded.

Gurmit stepped out of the hut into the small rain and lifted the backside of the clipboard over his head. He heard wailing behind him. It was Cho's son. He pressed the clipboard down hard on his skull to drive away the sound and jogged down the path to collect his third signature and end the day.

In the staff compound, he saw Miss Tu and Miss Chong, two Vietnamese English teachers at the Zone F school, bent over a red plastic tub, scrubbing underwear under Bobbi Sortini's clothesline. A pile of her clothes lay in a bucket behind them. Bobbi was sitting on the porch of her yellow bungalow, eating. She looked out at the ocean with an air of preoccupation, as though enraptured by an internal symphony.

"I have been thinking about the table," he said.

"How I envy your private life," said Bobbi.

"And I am carrying something you have given away," he said. He pulled the T-shirt from his belt and draped it over his arm. He would make her understand how upset he was. He would scold her for stealing the T-shirt, and she would make it up to him by signing the report.

Bobbi looked at him blankly.

"Thank you," she said. "Are you a waiter now?" She smiled broadly. "I'm joking, for God's sake. You have such a hangdog expression."

"So much to do today," he said. He wiped the rain from his cheeks.

"Yes. You and your friend Mr. Ahmed of Task Force have some sleuthing to do."

"That is why I stand in the rain to talk to you," said Gurmit.

"Oh, poor Gurmit. You don't have to stand out there, you know," she said.

"What I have to say is very brief," he said. "Can only stay a moment."

"You're not disturbing me at all," she said, and took another bite.

"No?" said Gurmit. He shook the T-shirt at her like a cape.

"You're not disturbing me," said Bobbi.

"I am not disturbing you?" said Gurmit. He gave the T-shirt another shake.

"That T-shirt is very nice. Wouldn't it look better on someone's back?"

"Mr. Cho in Zone D says you gave it to him, isn't it?" he said.

"What did he say exactly?"

"He said you gave it to him."

"Are you sure?" said Bobbi. "I didn't give it to him for *him* to wear. I gave it to him for his *son* to wear. Who was wearing it?"

"That is not my point," said Gurmit. "This belongs in Supply."

"How long do you and Mr. Ahmed intend to keep the shirts clean in Supply?" she said.

"That is not what I am saying," said Gurmit.

"So take it back to Supply," said Bobbi. She speared another bite from her plate.

"You are eating fish," he said.

"It makes a wonderful breakfast."

"Lungfish?" he asked.

She swallowed. "Lungfish. No, not on this plate."

"Sunfish?"

"Excellent detective work," she replied. "Bite?"

Gurmit shook his head. "How are you having sunfish?" he asked. "None has come for weeks."

"Oh, Gurmit, really," she said sharply, and laid down her fork.

"You have received it from illegal fishing."

"That," she said, "is a beastly rule. How can you work with that Ahmed?"

"He did not make the rule," said Gurmit.

"Not us. Not the Viets."

"The head of Prison Systems," said Gurmit.

"Well, that explains it."

"You wish to register a complaint, isn't it?" said Gurmit.

"Not if I have to talk to that . . . what's his name? Encik Rawli?"

"What is the nature of your hesitation?"

"No hesitation," she said. "I just don't want to talk to one of those people."

Her hand twitched—in disgust, Gurmit supposed. Her bloody arrogance. He frowned. "Do you know how many refugees are drowning from fishing here this year?" he said. He fumbled for the figures swirling in his head. "Six." He was fairly certain he was correct.

"If they had more rations they wouldn't go fishing," Bobbi said.

"That is a different issue," said Gurmit.

"It's the *same* issue, Gurmit. It's called food."

"I am knowing the word," said Gurmit.

"Yes. I apologize. Of course you do. All I know is that they go fishing no matter what rules your friends make. Did you know my Zone F blackboard was stolen last week? Again? They're probably fishing right now, out there." She waved her hand vaguely in the direction of the ocean.

"You are assuming so much," said Gurmit.

"You see," said Bobbi. "Oh, I don't know how to explain it to you. I don't *know* know they're fishing now. But I *know* it, like I know Canada exists. That would be like your Thailand, except north of the U.S. I've never been to Canada, but I know enough about it that I believe it's there. Same thing with fishing. I've never *been* with the Viets when they fish, but I know enough about them to believe they're doing it. Can you understand that?"

"Yes, understand-*lah*," said Gurmit. "Is not so difficult."

"So why are you playing sheriff?" said Bobbi, spearing another bite.

Gurmit charged up the stairs.

"No fish," he said firmly, placing his clipboard on the bungalow railing. "That is the rule."

"If you'd care to wait," said Bobbi, brightening suddenly, "you'd see that I'm going to give the leftovers to Miss Tu and Miss Chong when they finish the washing."

The two women looked up at the mention of their names and waved. Bobbi waved back.

"And it is *so* delicious," Bobbi said.

"No fish, no T-shirts, no pictures," Gurmit said, mopping rain from his forehead. He suddenly realized what he had said.

"Pictures," said Bobbi. "We can't take photos now?" She folded her arms and looked straight into Gurmit's eyes.

"Never mind-*lah*," said Gurmit. "That is other business. No fish. No T-shirts. But I will close my eyes this time." Gurmit closed his eyes in demonstration. "Ahmed does not need to know."

"Oh, *tell* him. I don't care. He can try and kick me off the island all he wants."

"You do not mean that," said Gurmit.

"I suppose not," said Bobbi, folding her arms. "You know what your problem is?"

Gurmit busied himself with draping the T-shirt over the bungalow railing and pretended not to hear her question. He pulled the cloth to flatten it, and laid it over the wood to dry. He did not want to hear what Bobbi thought his problem was. He did not want to hear another word from her.

"I am needing your signature," he said, holding up the clipboard like a shield.

Bobbi unfolded her arms and took the clipboard from him. Gurmit then reached into his front pocket and placed a green pen on the table, by her plate of fish.

"Oh," said Bobbi. "Oh, oh, oh." She smiled wanly at Gurmit. He did not like what he saw.

"Now I get it," she said. She placed the clipboard on the table. "Gurmit see no evil," she said, cupping her eyes. "Gurmit hear no evil," she said, cupping her ears. "Gurmit speak no evil," she said, cupping her mouth. "But Gurmit get my signature. Yes? You won't tattle about the fish and the T-shirt if you get what you want."

He shook his head. He saw Bobbi's mouth move, and he noticed the freckles on her arm. Out of the corner of his eye he saw Miss Chong and Miss Tu beat Bobbi's underwear against a scrub board. Farther up the beach, a crowd massed under the awning of the hospital entrance, surrounding a man in running shorts who shot his arms up and down, as though raining down blows. The images froze in his mind, still as birds on a wire.

"Who are you to . . ." He couldn't bring himself to accuse her.

"All right then," said Bobbi. She scribbled her name in giant letters on the signatory line. She looked away when she had finished, as though resuming her internal symphony. She calmly rubbed her hands against her arms. "You can have something else too," she said, leaping up and entering her bungalow.

Gurmit heard a drawer open, then heard it slam shut. She came out immediately with a large rattan basket. Setting it on the table, she took her plate of half-eaten fish and shook it firmly into the basket. Slick globs of white flesh stuck to the sides of the plate. These she removed by deftly scrapping her index finger over the plastic surface.

"You get my signature," she said, handing him the clipboard. "And you get a fish." She thrust the basket at his face, briefly shaking it like a tambourine. "And you get a T-shirt," she said, grabbing the cloth off the railing.

Gurmit took it all: clipboard, basket, and T-shirt. He watched her turn and walk into her bungalow. Her hands were balled into fists, turning her knuckles the color of alabaster. His mouth opened, but he could think of nothing to say. And then he heard boys blowing palm fronds, trumpeting nine in the morning. So late, he thought. So bloody late. That was all he could think.

Days passed. The water barge made its weekly delivery; the rain let up. At dusk the generator in Zone C continued to sputter under its shed, and the Vietnamese mechanics handed their oily T-shirts over to the washergirls and yelled over the motor for their children to bring them packets of rice and fish sauce tied up in newspaper. Dragonflies settled on the shelters, and girls in white blouses giggled at their mothers and trapped the insects in jars. The debris of the day lay trampled on the footpaths: mangled cigarette packs, plastic bags, rubber bands, locks of hair around the outdoor barber chairs, the occasional rat-killing brick, a sandal here and there. And then it was night, just like that, the darkness glowing with coals and cigarettes, the lights from the Task Force barracks and UN compound bright and tinkly as carnivals. In the staff eating hut, the kitchen ladies served bowls of squid and cabbage and fried okra, placing them gently in front of the white people, away from the sagging hole in the middle of the red-and-white checkered tablecloth, then returning with a giant cauldron of steamed rice, which they held by the handles and dragged across the dirt floor on a wooden pallet attached to a rope.

Gurmit's seat was still empty. No one remarked on his absence. The staff joked about the sagging hole, moving their silverware about, playing shuffleboard games to see whose fork would come the closest to the edge. They drank coffee. They pressed the cool tin of the water cups to their foreheads. They ate with ravenous appetites, passing the bowls person to person, scraping their spoons against the metal, saying it sure would be nice if their table didn't look like a medieval map, where all the ships sailed into the pit at the end of the world.

Gurmit sat on a stump at the top of the Zone F hill, staring

down at the dark water and the mushrooming rainclouds racing in
from the mainland. With a pocket knife, he cut open a can bearing
a picture of a smiling sardine. He ate. At his back was the Zone F
primary school, all plastic tarp and saplings, where a woman stood
in lamplight, conducting English lessons. Gurmit wagged his head,
chewing to the rhythm of the students' chorus: *Hello how are you
I'm fine, hello how are you I'm fine.* He thought he could make out
faint lights far to the west, on the horizon, where Kuala Trengganu
would be, where beerbellied Sikhs would ride their motorbikes
through zones of chutney and cloves and turmeric. He inhaled
deeply, breathing in the moist night air, nostrils flaring, and he
pictured himself with them, riding the streets of the city, groggy
from beer and a dinner of *pratha* and chicken, putt-putting down
the middle of Bungaraya Road, by the tiny mosque, hooting at the
Chinese shopgirls clacking their heels on the walkways after a full
day at the emporium.

The image had weight; it was fleshy and breathing, and it filled
him with longing. He sat thinking about it later that night, sitting at
his desk in the office, catching up on refugee arrival and departure
forms. He had not been in the office for days. Miss Phu had simply
carried folders over to his bungalow, waiting quietly while he
stamped them or approved them or shook his head "no." He worked
dreamily now, pausing long moments, wishing with all his heart he
were off the island and back in Kuala Trengganu. The image seemed
so real he stuck out his hand, fending off an imaginary waiter bearing smelly food. He sniffed. Then he called himself a fool. The
odor was real. There, next to the plank, covered with his clipboard
and report, was the basket Bobbi had given him. The half-eaten
fish had turned rancid; the oil had stained the envelope and the
T-shirt; bits of flesh speckled the clipboard. He stopped working.
He tapped his pen on his desk. He looked around. "Ruin," he
whispered.

Rats were beginning to drop to the roof and chew at the plywood
walls. The fluorescent light was sputtering; geckos waited in stony

anticipation, like refrigerator magnets, along the length of the tube. Ruin. The whole office: the *India Today!* magazines, the jackfruit rinds, the soft drink bottle on the bench. Dustballs roamed the corners, moving with the faint breeze rising from between the floorboards, and to his eyes they did not seem to be dustballs at all, but the swirling, gaseous matter of ruin.

When the overhead light crackled, he groaned loudly and only with great reluctance stood up on his chair to jiggle the tube back and forth, scattering geckos across the ceiling. The tube glowed in his hand. It crackled off and on, and there in the light, as he stood with his feet on the chair, he saw a shadow fluttering on the front wall, something jerking and huge, and in his tiredness he was so startled by the sight he felt his knees buckle. He jumped to the floor, suddenly weak, and nearly toppled over. He felt himself floating, buoyed in something warm and dense, and then he was on his knees, falling hard, and his eyes were stinging. He clutched the chair, and then he felt it: a pressure on his shoulders, something frantic and hot, like hands clawing.

He crawled to his desk and pulled open the bottom left drawer, fumbling under his captain's hat. He raised his hand from the drawer, clutching a blue squirt gun, and fired an arcing stream of Raid wildly over his shoulder.

Nothing. The pressure was gone. He was squatting on the floor in a room of wood and paper and air. Overhead, the geckos slithered to the corners. A cockroach appeared, scuttling toward him across the ceiling. He was alone. He settled into his chair, facing the front wall, and tipped back slowly. He smoothed the lapel on his jacket, humming, just to hear the sound of his own voice, and cradled the gun in his lap. He couldn't stop shaking. He sat awhile, rocking, eyes roaming the walls, and then he balled his hand into a fist and brought it down hard on the desk. He clenched his teeth and rose. He raised the gun. He squirted insecticide at the envelope. He squirted the T-shirt. He squirted the basket of fish, his clipboard, his report. His hand clutched the gun so tightly he heard the plastic crack. Liquid was bubbling down his wrist. He fumbled with the bottom drawer and yanked out his captain's hat. He squirted it. He threw it to the floor, and then he was at the plank, and he stared at the mutilation. *Nguyen Van Trinh.* The name was infuriating. He put his finger to the trigger. Insecticide spattered the letters, but when he saw the dark liquid trickle down the gouges he felt the hairs on his neck bristle against his collar, and he held his arms wide and cradled the plank, pressing it close to his chest, feeling the splinters sink into his hands as he stroked its back, again and again, whispering to the wood forgive me, forgive me, forgive me.

A
Private
Space

When Gary Martindale's dim and flabby older brother, Rick, left Tacoma for South Vietnam—he was going to be an infantryman in the Delta, a radio operator—Gary, nineteen, was given to understand that people from families such as his own invariably came to a mean and wasteful end. It was evening, and he was poring over chess books, preparing for the upcoming Washington State Chess Championship. Just that morning he had stood somberly alongside his mother and father at the bus station, saying good-bye to newly minted Lance Corporal Rick Martindale. But now, slightly stoned, still unnerved by what he had witnessed, he sprawled out comfortably on his bed, a magnetic pocket chess set on his pillow, a *Chess Informant #46* at his elbow, analyzing a brilliant innovation by Bobby Fischer, a move so profound it overturned in a single stroke decades of grandmasterly assumptions.

Stirred, perhaps, by Bobby's improbable victory over communal and ingrained ideas, he saw in his own dogged attention to the move an attempt to renounce the certain outcome of his brother's tour of duty, the certainty of which had struck him like a slap in the face that morning at the bus station. He began nodding. Out-

comes, he knew, toking thoughtfully, were echoes of their beginnings and middles. The trajectory could be traced, the trace illuminated, sources identified. If he was honest—and at such a moment, he acknowledged, how could he not be?—he had to admit
that Rick's beginnings and middles under the family roof com-
mingled with his own. Rick the sad sack, the lard ass, the twenty-
one-year-old lump: that they were related hardly seemed possible,
yet it was undeniably true. There was contamination involved, leach-
ing, a hoary and involuntary exchange of cells and fluids, DNA. Once
or twice Gary thumped his chess set for emphasis. He found himself suddenly teary. He stretched out his arms then, stiffly, as if for
embrace, and by this act gave form to what he had always known
but had never before confronted. At the core of their shared history, his and Rick's, were not the bedrock pillars of strength and
affection that family life was intended to promote, but a vast and
terrible nothing.

Incidental and, beginning in adolescence, of increasingly little
influence in the family's affairs, Rick seemed to conduct his daily
life just out of Gary's line of vision, like a TV flickering in the corner. Rick was, in effect, the *idea* of an older brother, not the older
brother himself, and like most things one step removed, even the
solidity of his physical mass seemed a gift from the minds of others,
from those such as he, Gary, whose collective will constitutes the
social and physical world. Like it or not, that was the nature of
things. Right or wrong was not at issue.

Still, shaking his head, Gary now affirmed that he had never
willfully obstructed Rick's forays into a wider, fuller existence. At
the same time Gary could not help but admit that he had at times
offered up Rick's life to unnamed deities in exchange for increasingly brutish rewards for himself, concluding during his junior and
senior years with sincere prayers for a richly pornographic hour
with Annie Hershberger, who lived in the Sorenson Trailer Park
and wore hot pants like no one else. For such acts, no court of law
could have or would have convicted him, true. There was, as well,

much to be said for asserting your rightful place in the world and for insisting upon the proper place of others. Winters, for example, Gary joined with neighbors Dan Bacha and Tim Underwood in grinding his brother's face into mounds of dirty snow. Summers, they jabbed Rick's fat gut with a rake handle until rosy welts bloomed on his skin in a lush, gardenlike patch. Once, making some point or other about weak chess players, Gary told some mocking Rick-story in front of Russ Rassmusson, the Tacoma Chess Club ratings-board leader and many-times Washington State Chess Champion. "You got your white sheep, you got your black sheep," said Rassmusson, shaking his head. "Then you just got sheep."

Gary could not have agreed more. Though his mother, Cindy, and father, Marion, had wondered aloud sometimes if the abuse Gary meted out was intended to punish the eldest boy for being unlovable, and though to Gary the word *unlovable* sounded foreign and hysterical, altogether inappropriate, he had never been able to restrain from noting, publicly and defiantly, a mewling lack in his older brother. This lack, this absence, was of concern not only to Gary but, he believed, to the entire community. By proximity and parasitic contact, Rick posed the threat of infection. He was a corruption, a distortion, a shrinkage, even, of the rigorous and unforgiving larger natural order.

Evidence: Rick was large-hipped, questionably muscled, possessed of soft pouty lips and luxurious brown hair; he wore thick, black horn-rims and blushed easily. When the sun slanted just so, flooding between pine branches, his cheeks sometimes turned so pink you had to wonder if he had applied a layer of rouge. He was no good with his fists, and he was grimly unresourceful—once, rather than figuring out he could go in the back yard behind a bush, he pissed his pants in the hallway when the bathroom door-knob broke and he couldn't get in. So when out of nowhere Rick would cry—and he cried all the time, a regular baby boo-hoo—Gary did not ask what was wrong. When they argued, Gary simply hit him, then watched in silence as Rick fell to the floor and spouted outrage, too slow to fend off blows, too stupid to shut up. They shared nothing, not friends, bikes, smokes, ways to steal change from vending machines.

But now in Vietnam, Rick was going to get the top of his head blown off, and when he lay dying in the elephant grass he would think to himself how loud the flies were buzzing today and how muggy the air had grown and how dizzy he felt, and maybe even how the voices of his platoon buddies hovering overhead brought him comfort and joy. He would not think of Tacoma or his mother or father, and he would certainly not think of his younger brother, Gary, who, that night, after admiring Bobby Fischer's brilliant new move, found himself shocked at his own tears when recalling the morning's scene at the bus station, when all he could think to do was shake his brother's hand and say, "Take care of yourself."

At such moments young men sometimes feel their spirits push out against their skin, held in check only by welling goose bumps and electrified hairs. And, in fact, at that moment of good-bye inside the bus station, Gary had very nearly left his body. The station smelled of diesel and rank toilet water. The green paint of the pillars had been inscribed with racial epithets, and on the pavement lay a naked plastic doll, beheaded and dirty. Behind the Martindale family, a greasy man in a trench coat, some lunatic, kept up a feverish banging on a trash can, then lifted the lid by its broken handle and spun the lid around, as if to make it fly. Rick was already gone from them, his face a failed mask of warrior calm. Cindy and Marion bore the look of children receiving punishment for crimes they did not understand, stunned and distant, not up to acknowledging what had come to pass. A million thoughts went through Gary's head, and they all seemed to circle like bees, busy and confused, as if trucked through the night and presented in the bright morning with a new and uncharted field. Gary's hand went up, bye, then Rick's paunchy form boarded the idling bus and settled deeply into the crinkly brown seat.

That settling, viewed from below, outside, nearly caused Gary to

cry out in alarm. The window framed the image: Rick frowning
and frizzy-haired in the heat; Rick's head suddenly sinking back—
Gary swore he could hear the bus seat exhale—as if into the wrinkled
palm of the Devil himself. The sight was so unexpected, so jolting,
as to seem removed from normal space and time. It wasn't exactly
a premonition that Gary experienced or even the moment of clar-
ity he had heard visited those blessed with higher orders of intelli-
gence and observation. It was a moment commonly experienced,
yet little discussed, that lit-from-within passage of time in which
you sense another you is present, another you that knows all the
ways in which this moment is a beginning to some things and an
end to others. Gary's other Gary knew, and thus Gary knew, that
brother Rick, burying his head deeper into the seat, receding from
sight bit by bit, was by this act meekly surrendering to a monstrous,
hurrying machinery of which real machinery was but a part. The
bus would race him to the airport, a plane would hurl him across
the Pacific, then a shuddering chopper would dump him onto some
flat, boring field—quick now, double quick!—so that someone,
some hurrying alien stranger, could shear off the top of his head
clean as an onion.

Surely Columbus, centuries ago, had experienced such a moment of awareness. Months of muscular, rude waves and empty,
gaping horizons, enormous and mushrooming heavens. Sky above,
water below. The cosmos growing, day by day. Then out of nowhere: a strip of island, a black smudge. *India,* Columbus reported
wrongly, but that couldn't have been his most immediate or most
significant thought. The smudge surely did not inspire in him the
objective contemplation of his commercial and scientific idea, the
verifiable end of a long train of inquisitive thought. The most immediate, and meaningful, response aboard his stinking and unhappy
ship must surely have been of awe, of helpless, fearful praise in the
presence of something strange and powerful. What that smudge
actually was made little difference, at least at first. Any number of
images would have sufficed: mermaids; a circle of jutting rocks; a

phalanx of futuristic skyscrapers; even fantastical apparitions, the guardians of the mystic Spanish universe. All would have burned into his mind with the intensity of a clapping, bubbling emotion, the unprovoked kiss of a girl you had just met, the curious, burrowing muzzle of an animal you didn't know was creeping up from behind. *I am small*, one thinks at such moments. *The story is in progress and cannot be stopped.*

That was how Gary felt on his way home. Shaken, vaguely embarrassed, he thought, If that's true . . . well, if that's how the world turns, then what difference does anything . . . what chance do I . . . ?

He threw himself into preparation for the state championship. His *Informants*, of course, but also *Chess Life, Schachmanty Bulletin, Modern Chess Openings* (5th edition), even *The Dynamic Caro-Kann Defense: A Monograph*—he searched their pages for blunders, traps, sacrifices, for secrets. He didn't want to think about Rick anymore. He didn't want to think about what was unfolding in front of his eyes.

The following week, Russ Rassmusson (Washington State Chess Champion, 1960, '62–'65, '67) phoned the Martindale household and invited Gary to be his training partner for the state championship, less than a month away. "I want you to be ready for some work," said Rassmusson. "No screwing around. Anything that's not chess, put on hold." Gary jumped at the chance.

Rassmusson appeared to be in his late thirties, compact and dark-haired, ruggedly handsome despite the small pits in his left cheek, pockmarks grown so smooth over the years they appeared to have been scooped by a tiny spoon. When he walked into the Tacoma Chess Club, heads turned, and when his fine-looking girlfriend (Rassmusson never revealed her name) strolled in occasionally to say hi, she sent electricity up everyone's spine. Regardless of the weather, Rassmusson always wore a long-sleeved, button-down shirt and a brown sport coat, an attractive and even necessary wardrobe, Gary thought, if you spent weekends hunched over a chessboard, alongside rows of the grossly ugly and fearful and inept, who also, bafflingly and unexpectedly—they are nothing like *me*, one thinks, they are aberrations—filled those nearby rows of tables and chairs, and said hello to you, and made howlingly stupid moves with their chessmen. An instructor of English at the community college, Rassmusson smoked Dunhills from a small, narrow cardboard box and claimed not to understand that a *tenny runner* was what kids in Tacoma called a sneaker, all of which gave him an air of rigor and sophistication, especially when viewed in the context of his polite but distancing lack of interaction with the aforementioned patzers and woodpushers—"fish," in chess parlance, the bottom-dwellers blind to the tricks being played upon them by the strong players above.

The club itself was in a small building downtown. It smelled of pipe tobacco and urine, and its rows of chess sets were said to have been specially constructed by a Pakistani craftsman for the 1960 Seattle World's Fair. The club's plate glass window, notable for its professionally painted giant knight and pawn, suggested an earlier era, one in which men wore fedoras and women listened to Benny Goodman on the radio. So, too, did the giant ratings board, a green-felted expanse of plywood, bolted to the wall, on which members' names and chess ratings had been written on white cards, in Magic Marker, and affixed by thumbtacks in order of chess rating; so did the heavy chairs and tables, made of fine burnished dark wood, and the long line of framed black-and-white photos, along both walls, of deceased and still-living world chess champions. There were, as well, bulky onyx ashtrays, purchased and donated, the treasurer said, by retired master sergeant Jim "Ju-Ju" Bowen at an airbase in Guam, and a stainless-steel coffee urn that seemed forever to be percolating. The linoleum floor, installed for free by immediate past vice-president D. Dzironky ("I am Dee," he said, in thickly accented English), was a serendipitous and pleasing rust and cream chessboard pattern.

The club was a home away from home, lovingly tended by the city's small but committed cadre, and sometimes late in the evening, fresh from a victory, Gary would rub his thumb on the glass of the framed pictures, searching for resemblances between himself and the former champions, whose likenesses seemed to stare back with a severe and regal sympathy. There was inside the club an air of calm and order. On the giant ratings board you saw your name and rating, and everyone else did, too. There were no secrets, no withholdings, and you spent your evenings knowing all you needed to know about the fish sitting across from you, or about the fish grimacing by the coffee pot, or about the fish striking the plunger of the chess clock too hard.

Even a cursory glance at the giant ratings board told you something very clear and important. Russ Rassmusson had been at the top forever. His card, occupying the first spot on the board, had turned yellow with age, and it still had no creases, no thumbprints, as if never touched by human hands. Rassmusson had been profiled twice in the *Tribune*; he had once received a complimentary hand-written note from a visiting Latvian champion; he had been elected unanimously to the Washington State Chess Hall of Fame. Recently, though, not all the talk was of Rassmusson. As any visitor in the past six months would have clearly seen, the ratings board had begun to reveal something new, something equally clear and important: below Rassmusson, in the second spot but well above the depressingly but unsurprisingly vast ocean of fish ("The poor, sayeth Jesus, shall always be among you," said Rassmusson), was the bright, well-creased card of Gary Martindale, the whiz kid rising so fast some fish once asked him if he was getting the bends.

Now, Tuesday and Thursday evenings and on weekends, Gary trained with chess master Russ Rassmusson. They played five-minute chess for quarters. They reviewed mating attacks with bishop and knight versus king, contemplated rook and pawn endings, studied variations and subvariations of the King's Indian, the Sicilian, and the Ruy Lopez. "Pay attention," said Rassmusson, snapping his fingers. "You've got to be *here*, not floating around." So Gary straightened in his chair. He watched Rassmusson take apart his Nimzo-Indian. Then he showed Rassmusson a gambit line in the French Defense; Rassmusson found a flaw immediately. They stayed until the buses stopped running.

Through it all, through the bitter coffee in Styrofoam cups Rassmusson brought along, Gary could not still his mind long enough to stop thinking about that awful morning at the bus station. He thought about it in roundabout ways. He thought, for example, about where the family lived. He had pulled a 3.0 GPA in high school without ever doing homework, and friends called him Brainiac (he had won the state high school chess championship his junior year), but he had no plans, and money was tight so he lived in his parents' attached garage, despite the wolf spiders in the shag rug by his bed and, especially during dry months, the bloated snakeflies that rose in the night to burrow into his mattress and deposit larvae. His parents' small home was in the south part of the city, at its farthest point, in unincorporated Tacoma. It stood on a rutted unpaved street where all the houses looked dark and in need of painting, and no one knew who was living next door.

Certainly the only time you saw couples at the threshold of their houses was when one was shoving the other out the door. Gary had witnessed such an event in the neighborhood three times. The man would be standing outside on the steps; the woman would be inside, half-exposed, grasping the knob, opening and closing the door quickly. *You give me nothing*, she'd yell, something like that. The man, silent and fuming, would turn and see Gary staring, then shout something equally loud toward the door, *bitch, cunt*, words to that effect, and walk quickly to the car and spray gravel into the sewage drain and go roaring down the road. The woman would then appear behind the living-room window, veins ballooning on her face, hands pressed white against the pane, shouting something Gary couldn't hear.

Why should such an event occur right in front of him three times? It defied statistics. How was it that, a few blocks down, in incorporated Tacoma, life proceeded along lines of generosity and fullness? It seemed a conspiracy of great natural forces, and, indeed, the city planners seemed to take great pains to reinforce the distinctions between incorporated and unincorporated Tacoma. Two blocks north of the Martindales, the vague and beaten unincorporated gravel road transformed into a glassy, thickly tarred street, marking entry into the incorporated sections of the city. There, a good rain made the houses shine, and the dew hung from shrubs like the sheer cloth you sometimes see on saintly women in religious paintings. The tucking in the brickwork was fresh, the windows clean, and the gutters were straight and cleared of birds' nests. Evenings, you could see middle-aged couples inspecting their marigolds and roses, bending plumply at the knees, their iced teas held at arm's length, like the tiny, pole-borne weights carried by highwire walkers.

Invariably Cindy would say, "Look at all this." His mother would be cornering, turning the steering wheel of their rusting Buick by tiny increments, keeping her hands in a ten-and-two position. "Everything's so nice," she'd say, sharply. Then she'd stomp on the gas pedal and speed home dangerously, running stop signs sometimes, once driving a girl on a bike into the curb. Had she always acted so crazy? Gary wasn't sure. He listened intently now from the passenger seat. He analyzed. She worked in a dry cleaners and smelled of dyes and wet wool. Most of the time she spoke in the swallowed monotone of someone used to being ignored.

"All the little cornish hens nice in a row," she said, roaring down the incorporated street. "*Look* at these houses." She had a thing about cornish hens. For years she had prepared dinners of cornish hens, four whole birds on four plates, and even when the family stopped having dinners together, sometimes Gary saw her at the table, sawing with a plastic knife and fork through the carcass of a freshly cooked cornish hen. They were perfect, she'd always said:

complete, separate, an entire creature in miniature. And it was true, you felt important when you ate one, like a giant. In a few quick bites you could swallow everything, limbs and breasts and neck.

Maybe, really, that's what she wanted to do. Every day she had to drive home in the Buick, down Marigold Avenue, then onto 70th, past all that perfection. Maybe she wanted to stride down those sparkling blacktop streets and devour tree and shrub and house, and maybe the fact that she couldn't made her tempt the laws of statistics. Maybe, when he thought about it, she saw in the line between incorporated and unincorporated Tacoma evidence of a hurrying, hateful machinery. Quick now! As fast as you can go. Double quick, out, out! In old photographs Gary had seen, black-and-white shots with wavy edges, she looked pretty and dark-haired. Now she wore a clear plastic cap around her head. Her face and arms looked drained of blood. She hardly ever seemed to move her eyes.

Gary had been blessed with certain attributes, a fine head of blond hair, a pleasant face, and a profoundly compressed belly—the result of a medical condition, the intestines slowly strangling the stomach, which of course made it not a blessing, but which, in his vanity, he fancied a guarantee that he would never suffer imprisonment in sludgy layers of fat. Rick, who had not been blessed with certain attributes, had always been blubbery, even after basic training, as were so many of the fish at the chess club. The club was always full of stinky fat men, and they moved slow as dray animals. There were cripples, too, men in wheelchairs and quiet, doughy boys who didn't like the sun; and there were blotchy alcoholics and bearded men who apparently didn't bathe. Occasionally, unkempt souls in dirty pants wandered in and helped themselves to the restroom in back. Months ago, Gary had looked on with approval when Mr. Finnegan walked in, Mr. Finnegan looking like Burt Lancaster, tall and athletic, well groomed, Mr. Finnegan, who might as well have spit in the coffee urn when he told Russ Rassmusson he was a machinist and out of work.

Now these men filled Gary with rage. Now he wanted them dead. "Quiet," he barked at a chatty newcomer. He picked up a pawn and cocked his arm, as if to hurl the chess piece at the offender's head.

"Oh, my," whispered Rassmusson. He reached into his pants pocket and much to Gary's surprise pulled out a folded Swiss army knife. "You'll be using this next if you're not careful." He quickly put the knife back into his pocket, then reached across the chessboard and placed a hand on Gary's arm. "Focus," he said, gently. "Just let them be. We all play the hand we're dealt."

Rassmusson's fingers seemed to burn into Gary's skin. He looked Rassmusson in the eye. What if, wondered Gary, the hand he had been dealt was in fact Rassmusson's hand? There were sources, traces, trajectories binding them together. He had known Rassmusson for more than a year. They were at the top, the lion and the cub. Rassmusson had *chosen* him, for Christ's sake. Rassmusson had the big talent, and maybe he did, too. In front of his friends Dan Bacha and Tim Underwood, Gary talked about all the money he had won in tournaments—local ones, to be sure, ones awarding twenty dollars for first, but officially sanctioned events, nonetheless. They called him a professional, and he never bothered to correct them. He had trophies on a bookshelf, checks to cash, and an inscribed certificate from the United States Chess Federation.

With Rassmusson as tutor, he might even win the state championship, might get his photo in the paper. At some distant point he might even *be* another Rassmusson, a man with a white-collar job, with neatly pressed clothes, a man with a presentable face and body, a fine-looking girlfriend, a sense of humor appreciated by others, a ready fund of knowledge about the world outside (coming in late one evening, Rassmusson had excused himself, saying he'd been working on the McGovern campaign). Once, Gary had smelled alcohol on Rassmusson's breath, but it had been late in the evening and near Christmas. The man presented a wonderful picture, and that night Gary had a flying dream. In the morning, he swore he would cut back on weed and the occasional chaser of speed, and cease masturbating altogether, at least until after the state championship.

But other days, walking in the front yard, Gary passed through patches of tall wet grass and felt the heavy moisture clinging to the blades. Tropical, he concluded. He squatted and ran his fingers through the foliage. He stared long and hard into the tree line down the block. It would be scary, sure, but wouldn't it be something to walk up behind Rick in some rice paddy and stick out his hand and tap Rick on the shoulder and say Hey. Wouldn't it be something? *Hey*, he whispered, and he stuck out his hand, shoulder height, tapping air. Hey. Hey, Rick.

In the house, his father, Marion, was always watching TV. "One boy in Vietnam, one boy here," Marion would say, tipping back a Schlitz. "One fights a war, the other plays chess. What you gonna do, sir? What you gonna do?"

Marion had always done that, had always mumbled to himself like an actor memorizing a script, but his question—*what you gonna do?*—became a mantra, at least when Gary was around. The mantra was hypnotic and for that reason powerful, especially when intoned, increasingly now, in front of Gary's friend Tim Underwood, who tromped through the living room with a folding chessboard and plastic pieces, intent on finally beating Gary in an offhand game, before they went down to the Sorenson Trailer Park, where they'd drive around, smoke grass, maybe scare some kids, see if Annie Hershberger was in her hot pants and wanted a ride somewhere. "You win the state championship," said Tim Underwood, "Hershberger'll do it with you. I bet you she will. Win that title, Brainiac."

"Oh, I will," said Gary, capturing another of his friend's chess pieces. "I'm on a mission."

Marion calmly wheezed, talking loudly from a chair in the

kitchen. Cindy sat across the table, watching Walter Cronkite on their small black-and-white. "Sir, what you gonna do?" said Marion to no one in particular. "You sir, that's right, you." He stared glumly at some point on the wall.

Looking up from the chessboard (he was already up a queen and a rook), Gary saw in Marion's narrow, blinking eyes the strain of a man struggling to hold back something. A judgment, perhaps. A summing up. Marion's words took on a menacing aspect, grazing Gary's ear like scattershot. This man, his father, bunched on the chair, working swing shift at the West Coast Groceries warehouse, sleeping through the day: had he always looked so weary, so baffled?

Gary, capturing another of Tim's chessmen, shouted out to Marion. "If I ever saw a gook here," he said, "I wouldn't want to be in his shoes." Gary then shook his head for a long time, signaling what he'd do to the trespasser was too terrible to tell.

Marion, sighing, got up and walked toward the refrigerator.

"Are you getting another beer?" Cindy said, turning from the TV.

"Yes ma'am," Marion said. "I'm getting another beer."

She watched him pull out a Schlitz. "So be my guest," she said. She shook her head. "Drink yourself silly. Do whatever you want."

Marion walked back to his chair.

"You know what I'd do?" Gary said. He looked up from the chessboard at Marion, then at Cindy. "I'd beat the shit out of a gook, that's what I'd do."

Marion got up and opened the door to the utility room. He rolled the cold can across his forehead and proceeded down the stairs.

Cindy frowned. "Gary," she said, "no swear words in the house." She balled up a fist, raised her arm slightly, then splayed her fingers, as if discarding something.

There's no trash like white trash, Cindy was fond of saying. Of late, she had begun to let her tossing motion say the words for her.

When did Gary start to worry the strain was too great?

We soar, but admit to only the plainest of sins. The two parts of that sentence are as close to an answer as Gary would ever find. The airiness of the first part is forever shackled to the mutters of the second, *soar mutter, soar mutter, soar mutter,* over and over so fast and so hard the oppositions threaten to break the middle. Things began to happen quickly, and for Gary time took on a fantastical, herky-jerky quality, though one with a pattern, with a movement forward. Time became like swimming, the water thunking against you, your face shining and clean, and then you plunge, upside down, driven for reasons you cannot say toward the sea grasses and sand, down into a strong-arming current that bullies you along wherever it wants to go.

Lance Corporal Rick Martindale was killed in action October 12, 1969, outside the village of Quang Ngu, known locally for its excellent rice wine. Cindy and Marion did not weep, at least not in front of Gary or the neighbors, trying hard, Gary heard them say on the phone, to be strong for their boy still there. It was that language— *we're being strong for our boy here—* Gary remembered most clearly, that Gary understood as proof of what had happened, words tread-worn and wrong, and, because tread-worn and wrong, terrifying. Cindy brought home dinners of Kentucky Fried Chicken; Marion mowed the grass three days in a row. There was a shopping trip: a tie for Gary, dress-up black shoes for Marion. Then Gary sat quietly in the back of the Buick. Lots of cars were parked in front of the church. Marion addressed Ken or Mike, some barking kind of name, and let hands rest on his shoulder. "We lost one boy . . . ," Marion said, miserably, vaguely biblical. His face seemed to collapse. "And we found the other." Cindy turned away and her shoulders began to tremble.

It was as though Marion had opened the wrong book, was quoting from the wrong pages. *What does that mean?* Gary wanted to ask, but didn't. *What are you saying?* In the car on the way back home, they all looked out the windows. Later, Cindy baked some cherry brownies—for the smell, she said; the smell always cheered her up—and Marion stood with her in the kitchen and put his arm around her waist whenever she was still.

That evening, Gary sat on his bed in the garage, stroking his new tie, which he declared to Cindy and Marion was his new favorite piece of clothing. The room had always been a mess, and now the mess and the poor light and the smell seemed an accusation. Behind the bed, on top of a dented ice cooler, were paper plates crusted with mustard and bits of pizza. Clothes lay in detergent boxes piled atop older, crushed boxes from which leaked glimpses of rags and garden gloves and mementos from his boyhood chest of drawers— a miniature stirrup, a plastic battleship, a Mickey Mouse clock, a baseball glove without webbing, objects whose original meanings, once affecting, had long ago faded away. His bookshelves, lines of planks and concrete blocks, had been stacked with dog-eared books and papers and journals with vaguely pornographic titles, *Der Schachspieler, 64, The Blackmar-Deimer, Pawn Power, D'Echecs Europa #23.* In front of him was a Dutch Masters cigar box containing his chess notes and tournament games; on the cement floor, croutons, a dirty glass, a mysterious white button, a few tooth-marked plastic pens, stains of indeterminate origin and color spreading toward the door in wavy explosions, like a map of ocean patterns. His tournament chessboard lay at an angle in one corner. His polished-wood tournament chessmen, greasy and dull, were scattered in another.

So he walked from his bed to the garage-door pulley and yanked the heavy door all the way open. He wrestled the metal garbage can outside into his room. He swept up with a push broom. He poured motor-oil cleanser onto a small space on the floor, the area in front of his bed, and he scrubbed the surface clean. He tightened the screws on a folded card table near the door and dragged it to the cleared space, then he wiped the table clean and placed his board and pieces in the exact center of the table. The board and pieces he wiped clean, too, rubbing until they gleamed, and on one corner of the table he carefully placed a new black pen, and on another he placed a new booklet of chess score sheets. He brought in a small wooden chair from the kitchen and aligned it in front of the table. The result was so perfect he found himself shy about touching the arrangement. When he finally sat down, straightening his tie, his heart was racing, and he nodded to himself, pleased at the bright, uniform chessmen and board, the clean surface of the table and floor. There was something comforting about it all, something quiet and powerful in the way the table and board and chessmen stood out from the rest of the room.

When he let his mother in—Cindy banged on the house-side door with a dinner tray of chicken—she handed him the tray and folded her arms. She nodded toward the table, toward the shiny chessmen and board. "It looks like a religious icon," she said, and Gary thought how strange it was to hear those words come from her—*religious icon*—words he had never heard her say before. Leaving, she brushed against his arm, and he nearly jumped. He hadn't felt his mother's skin in years. And more: she was of the womanly flesh he desired, though she herself did not possess that flesh. Her flesh disgusted him, and he was aware in a vague way of something he hadn't thought about in years: that he had wanted a sister, someone sexy and cooing, but also distant; a girl with breasts he wished to savor only from afar, a beautiful girl with long hair and bright lips, a narrow waist, long, slim fingers hanging a polka-dot dress from the shower rod.

Early the next day Cindy knocked on the house-side door and gave him a letter from a Pfc. Jerome Witte. "When you have a moment," she said, indicating the letter. She left for work. Pfc. Witte had been in Rick's platoon. He painted a strange, hagiographic picture of Rick, called him a hero, let the Martindales know Rick had uttered brave and decisive final words.

He said It don't mean nothing, Pfc. Witte wrote. *He was as tough as they come. Then he was taken by the Lord. I loved him like a brother.* Gary imagined the scene, Rick in the tall grass, laid out flat, his glasses probably bent at some odd angle. He would have said those tough words because he would have heard them somewhere, from his buddies, or a movie or two. He wouldn't have known what was happening. *It don't mean nothing.* As if some kind of bartering had taken place. As if all reasonable offers had been considered.

Later, after Gary and Tim Underwood smoked a few joints, they drove in Tim's pickup to the Sorenson Trailer Park and slapped around some black kid until he got on his knees and said he was a nigger. They waved around their nickel bag, and they got Annie Hershberger to go for a ride, and on the bluff overlooking the Narrows Bridge, Gary tried to fuck her hard, before she was moist, and made her yell Stop it, stop it *now.* Then they all drove back to the trailer park in silence, and Gary and Tim dropped her off and waved and made plans with Annie to have a picnic together up at Snoqualmie Falls someday.

"Something wrong?" Rassmusson asked him at the club. Gary was losing every training game, and the state championship was in two days. He was missing simple combinations, easy threats.

"No," Gary said. He looked around the room, at all the patient, sweaty men, all their mulish failure. "Just tired, that's all."

"Things OK at home?"

Gary nodded. When Rassmusson had asked where the hell he had been the past week, Gary had shrugged and said Sorry. He didn't mention Rick. Rassmusson, smiling, had made a joke of it: "So buck up, grasshopper," he said. Gary smiled back.

Every moment now, it seemed, Gary thought of his brother lurching down booby-trapped jungle trails. A picture formed in his head, and the picture wouldn't go away. Rick would be lying flat on a muddy field, and Marines would be kneeling around him, saying soothing words. The top of Rick's head would be gone, only Rick wouldn't know it, and no matter how hard Gary tried to change the picture, he could see only loose meaty things bunched around his brother's skull, and not the spirits or inscriptions of a holy nature he knew must be etched onto his brother's bones.

When he played Rassmusson now, his fingers lingered over the wooden tops of the chessmen. He held up the chessmen to the light and looked closely, squinting like a jeweler.

The state championship, held over two consecutive weekends, was played in the back room of the Arby's on Pacific Avenue. It was an eight-man round robin, winner take all—the title, seventy-five dollars, and a two-foot high engraved trophy. Gary lost quickly in Round One. In Round Two, Lawrence Dorfner, the eighth seed and an awful player, beat him decisively. "Good game," Gary kept saying afterwards. "Good game." When Rassmusson walked up, inquiring, they chatted a while, then all three, Gary, Rassmusson, and Dorfner, moved the conversation to the tournament director's table and stood looking at the other game results, on large sheets taped to the wall. Rassmusson did some calculating, and Dorfner nodded and wondered aloud about who would make the best match-ups for Round Three.

There was a pause. Gary said, "My brother just got killed in 'Nam. I couldn't concentrate."

Rassmusson and Dorfner looked at him blankly. Rassmusson then opened his mouth as if to speak, but only frowned. At the bus stop later, Gary saw two men in leather jackets and black pants. They were boisterous, swinging their arms expansively; one was swearing. It was chilly and drizzling, and their hair was plastered like helmets to their skulls. The men seemed far away as the moon, and for a moment nothing made sense; there was no sound, no substance to the bench he was sitting on, no smell, and all Gary could do was rise and address them. *Motherfucking cocksuckers fuck off go fuck yourself buttfucks.* He said the words so loud he closed his eyes and felt the spit run down his chin, and he stuck out his face. One of the men punched him hard, then they pushed him around some before walking away.

By Sunday of the first weekend, the halfway point, Gary was 0-4, no wins and four losses. Rassmusson approached him. He stuck a Dunhill into his mouth.

"What'dya say?" said Rassmusson, lighting up. "Nasty bruise you got there."

"We still got next weekend," said Gary. "I'm just having trouble concentrating."

Rassmusson smiled. He talked about cabins up by Snoqualmie Falls, about how beautiful the scenery was, how relaxing the pines. It was all the rainfall in the woods, he said. The entire region was in what the botanists called a rainshadow. "Good for what ails you," he said, and he put his hand on Gary's shoulder. He told Gary he was going up there tomorrow night with his girlfriend. Just to look around, relax. There was a two-bedroom cabin. So if Gary was free . . .

Gary shrugged. "I should bone up on my rook and pawn endings."

"A trip to the Falls," said Rassmusson. "It's on me. All expenses paid. It'd do you good to get away for a while. There shouldn't be too much rain. Plus you'll get to meet my lady. What do you say?"

Gary stuck his hands in his pocket. "OK," he said, sounding less enthusiastic than he intended. He pictured himself throwing his arms around Rassmusson. *Now,* he wanted to say. *Let's go now.*

The next morning they left in Rassmusson's car, headed to the cabin near Snoqualmie Falls. Rassmusson's girlfriend introduced herself as Tina. She was a pretty brunette. Her voice was surprisingly loud; she had a tinkling laugh. She, too, was an instructor—"just artsy fartsy stuff," she said—at the community college.

The air turned cold almost immediately, and Tina, fiddling up front with the heater, said she felt like an Arctic explorer. Gary agreed. He pulled up the collar of his jean jacket. It had been a wet fall in Tacoma, and moss was growing thick as honeycomb, creeping in wide sheets under everyone's shingles. Even in incorporated Tacoma, the earth stuck to your shoes wherever you walked, and for weeks on end you'd track wet clumps onto the linoleum. The leaves were everywhere, cars left thin trails of mealy debris on the roadways, and sometimes drivers couldn't stop because their tire treads were clogged. The car was like an icebreaker, said Tina, and they were sluicing through the icecaps. The *H.M.S. Bullpucky*, said Rassmusson, and Tina punched him lightly on the shoulder.

But it was true, driving out of the city, ghostly Mount Rainier floating high in the sky, soggy branches and earth and leaves everywhere, giant pines around you, there was a sense of racing toward something, not away, and the more all the familiar objects and machines and landscape fell away, the more you felt like driving farther. Up they went, the radio on loud, Gary in the back seat munching on tuna sandwiches Tina had brought. They passed giant white puffballs splitting open along the roadside, spores floating in the wind. They smelled basswood, saw fields of white, glowing birches. They roared past moccasin flowers, a swarm of moths, stands of pine and bigtooth aspen, a sheet of drowned squirrel corn on the pavement.

At the Falls, they stared for a long time at the thin white thread of water plunging dramatically from the rock face. "Nice," Gary said, happily. "Nice." The pines were straight and tall, and Gary shivered in the forest shade. Rassmusson pulled out a pocket flask and took a few swigs. Tina gave him a disapproving look. "My keeper," he said, and they giggled and hugged each other. At Tina's request, they all played cards on a visitors' center bench, then they each went for a long, solitary walk in the mushy woods. At the Falls Restaurant, they lingered in the souvenir shop. Rassmusson and Tina held hands. Rassmusson held up a postcard showing a dog smiling at a fire hydrant. "Now who would buy something like that?" he asked, and Gary said he didn't know, but it sure wouldn't be him. "Give me a blank card, any day," Rassmusson added. "Just a white sheet of paper."

That evening they drove to the town of Snoqualmie, where they ate cheeseburgers and fries, and on the way back Rassmusson made Tina squeal by claiming to close his eyes on the straightaways. Then Gary helped Rassmusson build a crackling fire in the living room fireplace. When Tina pulled out a bottle of red wine from her overnight bag, Rassmusson, laughing, excused himself and returned with two more bottles. "Russ," said Tina, darkly. "A jug o' wine, a loaf o' bread, and thou," said Rassmusson. They kissed.

It was warm by the fireplace, and Gary removed his jacket. "Aren't you hot?" he asked, noting Rassmusson's long-sleeved shirt. Rassmusson shook his head. "What's hot," he said, "is me beating you in speed chess." He ran back to the bedroom and returned with a chessboard and chess clock. Tina rolled her eyes and excused herself—she'd read in the bedroom, she said—so Rassmusson, winking, set up the chessmen and play began. He poured himself a glass of wine, to the rim, then a smaller one for Gary. Rassmusson was expansive, more solemn as well as funnier than Gary had ever seen him. He was talking nonstop and playing brilliant speed chess, all at the same time.

"You're going through a rough time," said Rassmusson, pouring them both another glass. "I won't lecture. I'll just say this. A little chess is like your own little world." He captured one of Gary's chessmen, then started chanting:

Burzy Wurzy was a bear,
Burzy Wurzy had no hair.
Burzy Wurzy wasn't very burzy,
Wurzy?

Gary frowned. "Those lyrics right?"

"It's just me and you here," said Rassmusson. "Who cares how all the fish want to sing it? Checkmate in three, by the way."

They started laughing, it was great fun, and the time passed agreeably, speed chess game after speed chess game, glass after glass. Rassmusson, calling himself a klutz, licked up some wine that had spilled onto his hand.

"Oh, my," Rassmusson said. Gary had launched an attack.

"Got you now," said Gary, sending his chessmen rampaging around Rassmusson's king.

Rassmusson shook his head. "I think you're painting your dick red and calling it a charlie pole."

What he said made Gary shift in his seat, but he laughed anyway. He was shaking a little, he felt so good.

"Chess and war," said Rassmusson. He opened another bottle. "Like two peas in a pod. Neither one makes a whole lot of sense. But I guess that's not news, is it?" He seemed about to say something more when Tina reappeared, looking spectacular in a red sweater and slacks.

"Russ," she said, "I forgot to tell you. I got a letter from a magazine last week. A rejection, but they said they wanted to see more stuff."

"She's a poet," said Rassmusson. He raised his hand over the chessboard, signaling they should stop the game.

"Don't make it sound so dramatic," she said. She turned to Gary. "I write poems and sometimes they get published. Sometimes not." She reached into her pocket and pulled out a folded piece of paper. "Here's my latest," she said, and she waved it near Rassmusson's lips.

"Let's hear," Rassmusson said. He poured himself another glass.

"I'm a little shy," she said, smiling at Gary.

"I like poetry," Gary lied. "I want to hear."

So she sat in a chair and cleared her throat. *My fingers are dark lies*, she read. Her voice was shaky.

"Sounds persnickety," said Rassmusson. He was drinking straight from the bottle. "Thumbs don't count?"

"Let me finish. You can't complain before the last line."

"I'm not complaining. I'm just pointing something out."

"Are you on the third bottle?" she asked.

"Depends. So what's the lie?"

"There are several of them."

"Several lies," he said, pleasantly. He turned to Gary. "Imagine that."

"Sweetie, I don't want to read the rest," she said, standing. She put the paper back into her pocket and sat down next to Rassmusson. "I'm interrupting your game." She draped her arm around his neck.

"The trouble is . . . ," Rassmusson said, pouring Tina a glass. "Well, here's the trouble. There are no actual lies in chess, and there's not the opposite, either. It's just a game, isn't it?" He took a swig from the bottle. "Now think about that. No actual content. That's really something to think about, isn't it?"

He pointed his finger at Gary and wagged it. "In real life," he said, "some facts are truer than others. Facts, my friend, are not all created equal. Some put a fist in your gut and set up shop right about here." He struck his chest, hard. "You know what I'm talking about, Gary? Well, I sure do. I got some facts for you."

"Sweetie," said Tina, quickly. Gary shook his head. He felt dizzy.

"OK," said Rassmusson. "OK. I'm just saying sometimes life treats you ugly, and sometimes you can just let it pass right through you. Like it's nothing."

"So what are you saying?" Gary asked. His voice was sharper than he had intended. "What are you talking about?"

Rassmusson stood, a bit unsteady, and, turning his free hand into a scythe, swept aside some chessmen on the board. The action seemed consciously theatrical, as if rehearsed, but Rassmusson's face was hard and red. Gary's shoulders tensed up. "I'm saying chess don't mean shit," said Rassmusson, "I put in twenty years on a *game*, that's what I mean. You might as well go spit into the Grand Canyon. Doesn't make a goddamn bit of difference."

Gary looked away.

"Russ, please," said Tina. Gary wasn't sure what happened next. There was a thud. He heard Tina cry out, and when he looked up he saw Rassmusson had lost his balance and fallen against the coffee table. Rassmusson was on the floor, clutching his head and rocking.

Gary leaped up to get a towel from the bathroom. "No," Tina shouted. She pointed to the front door. "Go out to the car. There's a first-aid kit in the trunk." Gary grabbed the keys on the counter and ran out.

When he returned with the small, plastic box, Rassmusson and Tina were squatting in front of the fireplace. It was dark—the fire was barely flickering—but Gary, stepping quietly, saw a rumpled quilt next to them. Rassmusson's shirt had been removed. Tina was dabbing his face with a sleeve. "Here's the kit," Gary said. He saw dark lines on Rassmusson's arms, then on his chest and stomach. He squinted. Rassmusson's eyes were closed; he was still clutching his head. Rassmusson's body was nearly hairless, and on the man's chest Gary saw the outline of a knight, then a bishop. Tina was rubbing one of the knights, by his left nipple. There was the outline of a pawn on Rassmusson's shoulder. Gary saw two rooks on his right forearm. His shoulders and arms appeared to have the outlines of pawns and kings.

"Russ," said Tina. Rassmusson opened his eyes. She grabbed the quilt and placed it like a curtain in front of him.

"Skin etchings," said Rassmusson. There was a dark patch on his scalp. He looked straight at Gary. "Like tattoos, OK?" He sounded angry. "That OK with you? You ever see Michelangelo's men in stone? I guess you wouldn't have." He let the quilt drop, then pointed at the ragged dark lines crisscrossing his stomach. "See this stuff?" The top of one of the knights seemed to be bleeding. "A Rassmusson original. That's a whole lot of nothing trying to get *out*, my friend."

Tina walked over to Gary, a never-mind smile on her face. "Time to turn in," she said in a sing-songy voice. "Thank you for getting the kit. It's got some iodine in it." Drawing close, she whispered: "Sometimes he gets carried away." Gary handed her the box, and without a word walked to his room and closed the door. He stood a moment, listening, then quietly locked it. He heard noises all night—whispered conversations, some thumps, a scraping like sand-paper. A heavy bottle clinked against something metallic. In the morning, he heard snores coming from their room. Underwear lay bunched outside their door. Wine in a drying red pool covered part of the floor where Rassmusson had fallen.

On the drive back, Tina slept in the front seat, Gary in the back. They stopped for a quick breakfast at the Great Northwoods Café, eggs and toast, lots of coffee, but mostly they were quiet, pointing every now and then at drivers in cowboy hats, once passing a soli-tary cow in a field. The silence was unbearable for Gary. It was as though time ceased, as though everything remained in a perpetual present tense, until someone spoke. Rassmusson felt it, too, Gary thought, and Tina. Pulling up to the Martindale driveway, Rass-musson got out and helped Gary rummage through the trunk for his jacket. Gary thanked him for the trip.

"I hope I didn't scare you away," Rassmusson said.

"That's OK," Gary answered. Rassmusson surprised him by shak-ing his hand.

"I'm dropping out of the tournament," said Gary.

Rassmusson looked at the ground for a moment. "Well," he said. "I'm sorry to hear that. I really am." He knew what Gary was saying. He knew they probably wouldn't ever see each other again. Then he was back in the car, waving bye with Tina, and they were gone, turning left on Marigold, toward incorporated Tacoma.

Inside the garage, Gary heard Cindy and Marion in the living room, watching TV. It was almost noon. Through the wall he heard the hollow sound of Cindy placing a coffee cup on the table, the squeaks of the couch when Marion sat. He listened for a while, then picked up the board and chessmen from the card table and shoved it on top of a case of soft drinks. Some of the pawns fell off, and he left them where they lay. He dragged the card table back to a dark corner, pushing it against the cleaning materials and air filters. He walked back to his bed, then heard *The Dick Van Dyke Show* come on. He stood, brushed off his pants, and walked through the door, past the kitchen, then into the living room, where Cindy and Marion looked up and smiled.

We are born in a caul of sin, and the world is a wicked place. But if you had said that to Gary then, he would have called you an asshole. The words were no revelation. They were not news. No clutter: that's what he was thinking. Back in his room, where the table and chessboard had been, was now a clear, empty space. It remained clear and empty that night, and the following night, and into the weekend and longer. Sometimes thin ropes of light streamed into the area from the top of the garage door or from the rafters, and sometimes he saw the dust illuminated—like floating planets, he'd think, like tiny aquatic life, and then he'd smother the thought, he'd shake his head at the fancy metaphors, the tricks. Still, he marked off the space from the rest of the room. He made sure it was swept clean. He assigned it secret names, Rickaroo, Rickereeni, Ricko-Micko, Ricky Ticky Tick-Tock, silly words he had never thought of saying before. Later, in a few weeks, he'd be a little high, nothing serious, and when he was ready, when it was quiet outside, he'd stick his hand into all that space, into a million miles of nothing, and he'd make a little tapping motion. He'd stick out his hand, shoulder high, into all that burning, wicked nothing, and he'd give a curt nod and say Hey. Hey, man. Hey.

PAUL EGGERS is a former Peace Corps volunteer and UN relief worker; he is also a former nationally ranked chess master. He received his Ph.D. in fiction writing from the University of Nebraska-Lincoln. His novel *Saviors* (Harcourt Brace, 1999) was a Barnes & Noble Discover Great New Writers selection and won the Maria Thomas Fiction Award. The recipient of a 2002-2003 National Endowment for the Arts Fellowship, he teaches creative writing at California State University, Chico.